DEATH OF A BACON HEIRESS

"Pork Chop, what happened to you?"

Hayley bent down to pet the pig, whose eyes were wide with panic.

As she reached out with her hand, the pig backed away.

But he wasn't frightened of her.

He was upset.

He waddled in the opposite direction, dragging the leash behind him.

Hayley stood up and followed him deeper into the gardens.

Pork Chop ran so far ahead of her she lost sight of him momentarily, but then she heard a wailing sound. It was an agonizing cry as if the poor pig was in pain. She followed the sound and came upon a muddy area where a sprinkler system was timed to shower the foliage and grass. There she saw Pork Chop circling around a body lying face down in a mud puddle.

It was a woman.

Hayley gasped.

There was no question who it was judging by the inconsolable behavior of Pork Chop, who continued wailing and snorting.

It was bacon heiress Olivia Redmond.

And she was very much dead.

Books by Lee Hollis

DEATH OF A KITCHEN DIVA

DEATH OF A COUNTRY FRIED REDNECK

DEATH OF A COUPON CLIPPER

DEATH OF A CHOCOHOLIC

DEATH OF A CHRISTMAS CATERER

DEATH OF A CUPCAKE QUEEN

DEATH OF A BACON HEIRESS

DEATH OF A PUMPKIN CARVER

DEATH OF A LOBSTER LOVER

EGGNOG MURDER
(with Leslie Meier and Barbara Ross)

Published by Kensington Publishing Corporation

A Hayley Powell
Food & Cocktails Mystery

DEATH OF A BACON HEIRESS

LEE HOLLIS

KENSINGTON PUBLISHING CORP.
http://www.kensingtonbooks.com

KENSINGTON BOOKS are published by

Kensington Publishing Corp.
119 West 40th Street
New York, NY 10018

All Kensington Titles, Imprints, and Distributed Lines are available at special quantity discounts for bulk purchases for sales promotions, premiums, fund-raising, and educational or institutional use. Special book excerpts or customized printings can also be created to fit specific needs. For details, write or phone the office of the Kensington special sales manager: Kensington Publishing Corp., 119 West 40th Street, New York, NY 10018, attn: Special Sales Department, Phone: 1-800-221-2647.

Kensington and the K logo Reg. U.S. Pat & TM Off.

ISBN-13: 978-1-4967-0252-4
ISBN-10: 1-4967-0252-2
First Kensington Mass Market Edition: April 2016

eISBN-13: 978-1-4967-0253-1
eISBN-10: 1-4967-0253-0
First Kensington Electronic Edition: April 2016

10 9 8 7 6 5 4 3

Printed in the United States of America

Chapter 1

Hayley Powell wished she was anywhere else as she picked at the last of her butter croissant and sipped what was left of her now cold coffee.

Bruce Linney was still talking.

Hayley checked the time on her cell phone. He had been prattling on for at least fifteen minutes. She sighed, brushed some stray crumbs off her light green blouse, and fixed her eyes on Bruce, pretending to at least be mildly interested.

She hated attending staff meetings at the *Island Times* newspaper.

Everyone gathering around a shoddy, scratched wooden table in a makeshift conference room with framed clippings of past landmark stories on the wall and discussing the major local news the handful of reporters were currently following.

A summer cottage break-in.

A controversial city council vote on new lobster boat regulations.

The high school swim team setting new records.

All topics Hayley was definitely interested in

hearing about. It was just that Editor in Chief Sal
Moretti, the big cheese at the paper, always scheduled these meetings during lunch, and he couldn't
resist chowing down on a pastrami and rye sandwich
during the meeting. Which was fine, but his mouth
was so full half the time he was unable to speak and
it provided crime reporter Bruce Linney with an
opening to hijack the proceedings.

Bruce loved to hear himself talk.

And today was no exception.

"Now, we don't know what kind of secret project
Dr. Alvin Foley was working on at the time of his
disappearance, but I am following up on a few leads
and hope to have some answers in the coming days,"
Bruce said.

Dr. Alvin Foley.

Now there was a fascinating story.

A young Stanford-educated scientist with an im-
pressive résumé who had moved to Mount Desert
Island three years ago to work at the Jackson Labo-
ratory, a leading genetics research center located on
the outskirts of town.

Single.

No kids.

Very quiet.

Kept to himself.

Exceedingly polite.

Hayley had run into him several times at the
Shop 'n Save, and he would always make a point of
smiling and saying hello.

He seemed to love cooking. He was always buying
exotic ingredients to experiment with new dishes.
One day it was Thai. The next Indian.

Hayley always felt guilty because she was the one who was supposed to be setting the culinary trends in town; after all, she was the paper's resident food columnist. But her grocery cart always seemed to be filled with Cheetos and packaged macaroni and cheese.

She hadn't seen Dr. Foley at the grocery store in a few weeks because he had mysteriously vanished without a trace.

No clues.

No evidence of wrongdoing.

But the rumors were flying around town fast and furious.

Kidnapping.

Extortion.

Murder.

Was he working on some kind of top secret medical breakthrough cure at the lab, and was someone willing to do him harm and steal his research in order to beat him to the punch?

That was the kind of rampant speculation everyone was gossiping about at the grocery store, at the high school baseball games, at the church socials. It was all anyone could talk about.

Hayley's phone buzzed.

She looked down at it, cradled in her lap, hoping it might be Aaron or one of her kids, but it was just Liddy confirming their girls' night out at Drinks Like A Fish, her brother's bar, after work.

Hayley felt a lump in her throat.

She was missing her kids big time.

Gemma was attending the University of Maine at Orono, studying for a bachelor degree in animal and veterinary science, and Dustin had recently been awarded a huge opportunity to spend the spring semester in Boston taking a college prep course in graphic design at the Massachusetts College of Art and Design.

She was so proud of them. But they were growing up so fast.

It scared the hell out of her.

She hated to admit she was suffering from a bit of empty-nest syndrome.

For so many years she had dragged those kids out of their beds to get ready for school, made them lunches, yelled at them to finish their homework. She had grown so accustomed to her roles as guardian, caretaker, and drill sergeant she was a little lost now that those roles no longer needed to be filled.

It was tough going home after work to an empty house.

She still had her loyal and loving dog, Leroy, and her demanding and moody cat, Blueberry, but it just wasn't the same.

"Now, I interviewed Dr. Foley's parents in Oregon and they said he had no enemies to speak of and was a dutiful son. They don't see any reason why anyone would want to hurt him. I put in some calls to Stanford and spoke to his professors and they all said the same thing."

God, Bruce was still talking.

This was not new information. Bruce had presented all of this exact information at last week's staff meeting ad nauseam. But he wanted to put on a good performance for Sal and show him he was still working hard on the case.

As for Sal, he wasn't even listening. He was opening his mouth as wide as he could to slide in the second half of his pastrami sandwich.

Hayley returned to her own thoughts again.

Aaron.

The handsome local vet she had been dating for a while now.

She had thought their relationship was progressing.

He seemed engaged. He was certainly affectionate.

But over the last month or so he had seemed to pull away.

She'd heard from him less.

He'd canceled a couple of dinner dates.

When she texted him or left a voice mail, he would take longer than usual to get back to her.

It was starting to worry her.

She had no idea where all of this was leading, or even whether this was the man she wanted to spend the rest of her life with, but she had grown so fond of him and didn't want to lose him from her life—

"Excuse me, Hayley, did you hear me?"

Hayley snapped to attention. "I'm sorry, what?"

"I asked you a question," Bruce said, scowling, arms folded across his chest.

"I didn't hear it," Hayley said, clearing her throat. "Could you repeat it?"

"Am I boring you?"

Hayley bit her tongue.

Don't answer that.

Don't answer that.

"I'm just a little distracted today, Bruce. My apologies. What was your question?"

"I asked you if you had any plans to investigate the Dr. Alvin Foley story," Bruce said, eyes fixed upon her like a laser beam.

"Why would I write about that? I'm the food-and-cocktails columnist. You're the crime reporter."

"Good. I'm happy to hear you're clear on that. Because my gut is telling me this is a big and complicated story, and we don't need some amateur sleuth sticking her nose into it and muddying the waters," he said smugly.

Muddying the waters?

Hayley couldn't even count the number of times she had jumped into a criminal investigation in the recent past and did Bruce's job for him. And she still let him take all the credit in his own column.

He should be on his knees thanking her. But she decided to stay mum. She simply nodded in agreement and let him continue his one-man show.

Hayley had zero plans to interfere with Bruce's fact-finding mission anyway. She was too preoccupied with her personal life.

Or lack thereof.

Besides, there was another story, completely unrelated to the strange case of the missing scientist, that was about to rise above the horizon.

And it was a doozy.

This one did not involve a missing person.

This person would be found very much dead.

Chapter 2

"I bet it's the Chinese government trying to steal our scientific research!" bellowed one lobsterman at the end of the bar at Drinks Like A Fish. "You can't trust 'em. Nope. Can't trust 'em."

And with that, the grizzled, bearded lobsterman downed his mug of beer and slammed the empty glass on the bar, signaling Hayley's brother, Randy, who was owner and barkeep, to pour him another.

Hayley sat on a stool at the other end of the long wooden bar, nursing a Jack and Coke and waiting for her two BFFs, Liddy and Mona, to arrive. She had finished work a little early and showed up at the bar to catch up on all the gossip with her brother before the girls arrived, but today's happy hour was particularly busy, and Randy barely had enough time to say hello.

"They got spies everywhere," another weathered fisherman said, nodding in agreement. "You just watch. In a week or so, maybe a month, a new doctor will show up to take that missing guy's place at the lab, and he'll be one of them. That's why they grabbed him. So they could replace him with one of their own and have all that top secret research at their fingertips!"

The other men, who were hunched over the bar and slurping their own warm beers, grunted and nodded their heads. They had a consensus.

Chinese spies were infiltrating Mount Desert Island.

That had to be the explanation for Dr. Alvin Foley's disappearance. Not that he had some kind of family emergency and had left town without telling anyone. Not that he hadn't liked his job and chose to quit without handing in a formal resignation. It couldn't be something so simple.

No. It had to be much bigger.

And none of the locals would be satisfied until they spotted James Bond parachuting onto Sand Beach from a passing plane to take out the nefarious evildoers bent on world domination.

Randy caught Hayley's eye and grinned. This was par for the course at his bar. Men out in tiny boats on the harsh, unforgiving sea all day hauling traps for meager wages enjoying some downtime by clouding their minds with alcohol and allowing their imaginations to run wild before returning home to their families.

Another bearded man, with a black cap and wearing overalls, sat at a table a few feet from the bar. He raised his own mug, clutching the sides with his pudgy red hands and dirt-lined fingernails. "I think you got it all wrong, bub. It ain't the Chinese. That's just crazy talk."

Finally—a voice of reason.

"It's the Russians!"

Never mind.

"The Russians can blend in better as long as they learn to lose the accent. Nobody would suspect 'em. You drop an Asian inside the lab and I'm already suspicious."

The fact that many Asian men and women already worked at the Jackson Lab apparently was an undisputed fact lost on these men.

The door to the bar flung open and Liddy hustled inside. She hurled her tote bag on top of the bar and slid up on the stool next to Hayley. "Sorry I'm late. I was showing a property to a couple from Brunswick who couldn't make up their minds. I hate wishy washy people. Just make a damn decision!"

Randy came over and smiled at Liddy. "What can I get you, doll?"

"Something sweet. Like a mojito. No wait. A daiquiri. No, I don't want to risk a brain freeze. How about . . . What are you drinking, Hayley? Oh, no, forget it. I don't want a Jack and Coke. Let me think. . . . Should I go simple and have a Rose Kennedy? But vodka gives me a headache. . . ."

Just make a damn decision, Hayley thought.

There was no way she would ever say that out loud.

"Where's Mona?" she asked.

"I saw her outside trying to find parking for that ridiculously big truck she drives. I know! I'll have a sea breeze. No. Make it a greyhound. I'm in a pineapple mood."

"You sure?" Randy asked.

"Yes. Wait. No. Yes."

"Greyhound."

"Yes . . ." Liddy said, still not sure.

"I'm going to go make it now, okay?" Randy said, backing away.

"You can always order something else if it turns out to not be what you want," Hayley suggested.

"You're right. Fine. Go make it, Randy."

Randy was already pouring from the carton of pineapple juice.

"Now what were we talking about?" Liddy asked.

"Wishy washy people who can't make up their minds," Hayley replied.

"Right. God, I wanted to shoot myself. How does anybody deal with people like that?"

The lobsterman with the weathered face who had first proposed the Chinese spy theory was now wagging a finger at the man seated at the table as he downed yet another beer, white foam settling into his thick, shaggy beard. "Of course, it could also be Middle East terrorists! The Jackson Lab is a prime target for those nut jobs. Just think what would happen if they got their hands on some deadly airborne virus. They could just pop open a vial and let the wind do the rest. Bar Harbor could be ground zero for a bioterrorist attack!"

"What the hell are they talking about?" Liddy asked, stirring the greyhound cocktail Randy had just slid in front of her.

"Don't ask," Hayley said, shaking her head.

Mona burst through the door, red faced and eyes blazing. She marched over and struggled to lift her bulky frame up onto the last remaining stool alongside Hayley and Liddy.

"Sorry I'm late. Liddy stole my parking space!"

"I did no such thing," Liddy said, setting down

her drink. "Oh, this is too sweet. I'm going to order something else."

"I pulled my truck ahead to parallel park it in the space right out front, and Liddy came roaring up behind me in her fancy Mercedes and just pulled in and took it. I had to go park behind the drugstore."

"I was doing you a favor, Mona. There was no way that monster truck you drive was going to fit in that tiny little space. You would have taken the front bumper off Hayley's car in the space behind it and right now you'd be on your knees begging her for forgiveness."

"There was plenty of room for my truck. You were just being your usual selfish, everything-is-mine self!"

"Well, at least you're both here now," Hayley said, hoping to calm the situation.

"That is so typical of you, Mona, pinning your bad decisions, like buying that gas-guzzling crime against the environment monstrosity, on me! Well, I won't have it."

So much for calming the situation.

"Oh, and I suppose that expensive Mercedes *you* tool around town in runs on cow dung?" Mona screamed, waving her hands at Randy to bring her usual Bud Light.

Hayley knew the only way to stop the sudden escalation of Liddy and Mona's latest diatribe against one another was to take drastic action.

Like dropping a bomb.

And that's exactly what Hayley decided to do.

"Aaron's going to break up with me."

Liddy and Mona stopped yelling at each other instantly.

"How do you know?" Liddy gasped.

"It's just a feeling I have. He takes so long to return my calls and texts. We hardly see each other. We had dinner a week and a half ago, but that's it. He says he's busy with his practice, but I think it's more than that."

"Have you talked to him about it?" Mona asked.

"I'm working up the courage. I think I'm avoiding a conversation because I dread how it might end."

"Honey, you could be misreading this whole thing," Liddy said. "Sometimes when a man suddenly pulls away, it could mean a number of things. He could be telling the truth and he's just busy, or he's dealing with a personal problem he doesn't want to drag you into. . . ."

"Or he really is getting ready to dump you. . . ." Mona offered.

Liddy grimaced and shook her head. "Or . . . there is another reason he may be avoiding you, and I have seen this happen so many times. There is the possibility that he's getting ready to . . ."

Her voice trailed off.

"What, Liddy, what? Getting ready to what?" Hayley cried, unable to take the suspense.

"Propose!" Liddy screamed at the top of her lungs.

She was so loud the gaggle of fishermen stopped their heated discussion about Chinese and Russian spies invading Maine and turned to see what all the fuss was about at the other end of the bar.

"Now, that's just ridiculous. . . ." Hayley said, laughing it off.

"Think about it. You've been dating a while now.

You've both expressed your feelings to one another. Gemma's already at college and Dustin has one foot out the door, so there's no awkward stepfather drama to deal with."

"Mona, help me here. . . ."

"I think she may be on to something," Mona said, shrugging.

Et tu, Mona?

Hayley couldn't get her mind around the idea of Aaron proposing. It was way too soon. And she wasn't even sure how she felt about the prospect of getting married again.

She had already failed spectacularly once. She wasn't ready to dive in again.

Or was she?

Part of her was excited.

Part of her was scared out of her mind.

And part of her was supremely skeptical.

A proposal? That couldn't be it.

Or could it?

It would be a miracle if she got any sleep tonight.

As Liddy breathlessly detailed her theory as to why she was right about this, Hayley noticed Mona nodding, totally on board with Liddy's thinking.

Liddy and Mona agreed on something.

Now that was the true miracle.

Chapter 3

Hayley was convinced she hadn't heard right as she clutched the phone to her ear. "I'm sorry, could you say that again?"

"We want you to fly to New York and appear on our show *The Chat*," the man's very calm voice said on the other end of the line.

How could he be so calm?

How could anyone be calm?

The Chat was a nationally broadcast talk show on a major network.

And this man, whose name Hayley had already forgotten, maybe it was Dan or Don, was calling her at home inviting her to New York?

Maybe this was a joke.

Did Mona corral her husband, actually get his butt off the couch, to pretend to be a big time TV producer in order to pull a fast one on her?

"What did you say your name was again?"

"Doug Hornsby. I'm a talent booker and we are doing a weeklong cooking segment, a salute to bacon, and your name came up as someone who could perhaps prepare one of your signature bacon dishes on our show."

Bacon.

Hayley had been inexplicably drawn to writing about bacon lately in her column. She chalked it up to a recent craving, but on some deeper level, she knew it was about her kids.

Gemma and Dustin loved bacon, and though she supplemented it with a lot of fruit and vegetables, she loved to indulge her kids with the sizzling breakfast staple every so often.

And bacon wasn't just for breakfast anymore.

She had been experimenting with all kinds of mouthwatering recipes.

A freshman psych major could conjure up some rudimentary theory to explain why she was so obsessed with bacon as of late. She missed her kids desperately, and bacon frying in a pan or the smell of bacon wafting from a casserole in her oven was comforting. It reminded her of them, like they were at home with her about to dive in to their mother's latest potato bacon casserole, or BLT sandwich, or homemade bacon pizza.

"Mrs. Powell, are you there?" Doug Hornsby asked, breaking the silence.

"Yes, I'm here."

If this was for real, if Mona wasn't on the other end stifling a guffaw, elbowing her husband to keep the joke going, then this was a twist Hayley definitely did *not* see coming.

When she'd arrived home from Randy's bar, the house had been dark and chilly, the temperature outside low for a late spring evening. Hayley had warmed up with a cup of hot chocolate and tried calling her kids.

She'd gotten both their voice mails. She didn't leave them messages. They would call when they had a free moment.

Or at least she hoped.

She'd debated calling Aaron. Just check in to see if he was having a good week.

Then she'd decided against it.

She wasn't going to throw herself at him. If he wanted to see her, he could pick up the phone.

Her shih tzu, Leroy, had scampered into the kitchen, wide eyed and excited to see her, but once she poured some kibble into his paw print bowl, he shifted his focus to his food and ignored her completely. Once the bowl was licked clean, he'd trotted into the living room to jump up on the couch he wasn't supposed to be on and nestled into his favorite silk pillow. Hayley had relaxed the house rules considerably with the kids gone, and both her pets were taking full advantage of her leniency. Her giant fur ball Persian cat, Blueberry, was undoubtedly upstairs curled up on her bed, wallowing and purring in the three-hundred-thread-count sheets from the Martha Stewart Collection Hayley had splurged on and ordered online from Macy's when she received a slight pay increase the previous month.

When the phone had rung, it startled her. She was just sitting in her oversized recliner in the dark, fingering the TV remote, not even sure she wanted to turn it on to try and find something to watch.

At first she'd thought it might be one of the kids calling her back.

Or Aaron.

But she hadn't recognized the number. 212. Was that New York?

She'd assumed it was just a telemarketer and wasn't going to answer it. But she was sitting in the dark with an empty mug and staring at her walls.

Why not see who it was just for kicks? It was something to do.

"Hello?"

And that's when she met the disembodied voice of Doug, the booking manager for *The Chat*, a show she watched religiously whenever she was home sick or had the day off. The panel was made up of three prominent women, a former newswoman, a comedic actress, and a lifestyle expert. They would open each show with a freewheeling discussion about the major news stories of the day and then segue into celebrity interviews, shopping tips, and cooking segments. It was a breezy, fun way to kill an hour, and the show was a ratings success for the network.

Doug was still talking.

"We had a Food Network personality booked, but her son got the measles and she had to drop out. We need a fill-in and your name came up."

"How on earth did you find me?"

"Rhonda's a fan," he said.

Rhonda.

Rhonda Franklin.

The comedic actress on the panel.

She was a larger than life, boisterous stand-up comic turned actress who had starred in a few Hollywood blockbusters, headlined her own sitcom for five years, and worked tirelessly to bring attention to the causes she was passionate about, like breast cancer and domestic violence. She was big, bawdy, and made a lot of noise whenever she mouthed off about anything. Hayley was an unabashed fan of the sometimes controversial but always hilarious woman. Especially when Rhonda had made the bold move to come out of the closet as a lesbian years before gay marriage was even the norm. It was a risk to her career, but in the end, it just made her more famous.

"You . . . you said Rhonda is a fan?"

"Yes. She's visited Mount Desert Island for several summers now and calls it her second home. The last time she was there she subscribed to your paper, the *Island Examiner*. . . ."

"Island Times."

"Right. Anyway, she discovered your column and now she never misses it."

This was too surreal.

And this phone call couldn't possibly be Mona playing a prank because even she wouldn't go so over the top and say Rhonda Franklin was a loyal reader of her small town food-and-cocktails column.

Nobody would buy it.

"I'm in a bit of a bind, Hayley. We need to fill the spot ASAP because we're running out of time, so can you commit?"

"When did you say I need to be there?"

"The show tapes Friday."

"This Friday as in . . . ?"

"The day after tomorrow."

Hayley's head was spinning.

What would she wear?

What about her frizzy unruly hair?

And her pale, drawn face?

The show must have professional makeup artists

and hair stylists and costumers to deal with frumpy single mothers who showed up on the set with no TV experience.

Or at least she prayed they did.

But Friday?

"Just say yes. Please. I can have our travel person call you back in five minutes to work out your flight details. We'll treat you well, Hayley, I promise."

"Yes."

She heard Doug let out a big sigh of relief on the other end the phone.

Hayley wasn't concerned about taking the time off work. She had a few personal days stored up. And Sal would probably be over the moon that she would be on a big time national TV show talking about his paper, the *Island Times,* and not their rival publication, the *Bar Harbor Herald*.

Doug thanked her profusely and hung up.

She still held the receiver to her ear.

She was in a state of shock.

And blissfully unaware of what fate was about to bring.

Chapter 4

Hayley wasn't exactly sure if Liddy and Mona had insisted on accompanying her to New York City to her first ever TV show appearance in order to support her and keep her nerves in check or for their own personal reasons. Liddy made no secret that she was overdue for her biannual shopping trip, and Mona was upfront about wanting a break from her hell-raising, obnoxious, out of control brats.

Her words, not Hayley's.

But as they waited at the baggage claim carousel at LaGuardia Airport after a harrowing thirty-minute connecting flight from Boston on a puddle jumper that rattled and shook from unexpected turbulence, forcing them to down straight shots of bourbon to stop themselves from crying, Hayley was happy they had made the trip with her.

Liddy, the seasoned traveler, had already secured a luggage cart for her three large pieces. They were in the city for four days, but Liddy seemed to have packed for a six-month world tour. Her matching baby blue Lipault Paris bags were the first ones out of the chute because she was, in her words, "a privileged frequent flyer with perks including unlimited priority baggage tags." It was only a few minutes before Mona's army duffel bag and Hayley's scuffed and torn years-old American Tourister were sliding down the conveyor belt. They exited the security doors to the main lobby of the terminal where Hayley spotted a wiry Hindu man in a tight-fitting black suit and tie waiting for them with a printed sign that said, HAYLEY POWELL & COMPANY.

"And Company? Why do I suddenly feel like we're the Supremes and you're Diana Ross?" Liddy scoffed.

"Because I only told them you were coming this morning and I didn't even get a chance to give them your names," Hayley said, waving at the driver, who scooted over to them with a wide smile.

"Welcome to New York. I'm Samir. Please, let me help you with your bags to the car."

Liddy was only too happy to hand over the cart to Samir while Mona eyed him suspiciously. They stepped outside and crossed to the lot directly opposite the terminal where they were escorted to a long black stretch limousine.

"Now, wait just a minute. How much is this going to cost us?" Mona barked. "I read online that New York cabbies like to jack up the price and overcharge tourists."

"Oh no, ma'am, I am not a cab driver. I work for a private company and the car has already been paid for by the network."

Mona still wasn't buying it. She was convinced this was a con job.

Hayley rifled through her bag for the printed e-mail she had received from the travel agent at *The Chat* and handed it to Mona. "Look, Mona. All expenses will be paid including lodging and transportation to and from the airport. They're covering everything."

Mona relaxed a bit. Samir tried to open the back door of the limo for Mona, but she pushed past him and slapped his hand away. "I am perfectly capable of getting into a car myself, thank you, in case that costs extra."

Liddy rolled her eyes, embarrassed, and climbed in after Mona as Samir popped the trunk using his remote key and began loading the bags inside.

Hayley couldn't believe they were actually here. It had all happened so fast.

She was grateful that Liddy had used her accumulated mileage to snag two free tickets for herself and Mona. She couldn't imagine experiencing this on her own. Especially since she had been feeling so lonely lately with the kids gone and Aaron so unavailable.

As she ducked into the car to join Liddy and Mona, she gasped at the opulence of the plush leather seats, glass bowls of candy, and fully stocked bar. Liddy was already pouring herself a cocktail.

"Help yourselves, ladies, it's going to be at least a forty-five-minute ride to the hotel now that it's close to rush hour," Liddy said.

Mona poked around the tray full of tiny liquor bottles. "I don't see a card with drink prices."

Liddy sighed. "It's complimentary, Mona."

Mona hesitated, but quickly got into the swing of things and was excitedly screwing off the cap on a blueberry vodka sampler while downing a fistful of pretzels.

Samir put on some soft music and they were soon crawling along the Grand Central Parkway toward Manhattan.

Hayley took in the spectacular view of the New York City skyline. It was dusk and there was a golden hue washing over the skyscrapers, making it seem like some magical urban Oz.

Hayley had been to the city before, when Randy was trying to make it as an actor, but he had lived in a tiny fourth-floor walk-up studio in a seedy building near the meatpacking district, so she was anxious to experience New York on a slightly grander scale. She wasn't disappointed when the car finally pulled up in front of the Le Parker Meridien, a luxury midtown hotel on Fifty-sixth Street. A uniformed porter whipped open the back door of the limo and offered a cheery welcome, startling Mona, who was now slightly tipsy from her vodka samplers.

They piled out of the car and thanked Samir as two more porters attended to their luggage.

They were led inside to the large ornate French-inspired lobby.

Liddy, who prided herself on her well-heeled tastes and called herself a "five-star girl" when she traveled, was duly impressed but tried to mask her awe as they ambled over to check-in.

The handsome young man behind the polished and modern desk had a slight French accent; Hayley couldn't decide whether it was natural or put on. He was very helpful and friendly, especially when patiently explaining to Mona that all incidentals including room service would be covered by the network. Once that finally sunk in, Mona was insisting they eat in the hotel that evening instead of going out to one of those fancy high-end restaurants that even charged for a hunk of bread and a slab of butter. If the TV bigwigs were springing for free food in the room, why not take advantage of it?

Liddy, of course, protested. She was in New York. She had no intention of hiding in a hotel room, no matter how tasteful and luxurious, when the Big Apple beckoned just outside with its exciting nightlife and armies of single men.

"Now, we agreed before we left Bar Harbor that if there were any conflicts we would take a vote and majority would rule, so you have the deciding vote, Hayley," Liddy said confidently, knowing full well Hayley wouldn't want to stay locked up in the room on her first night in Manhattan.

They walked onto the elevator and Liddy pressed the thirty-eighth-floor button, and within seconds they went speeding up into the clouds.

There was a moment of silence.

Liddy eyed her warily. "Hayley?"

"Well, we are here for the whole weekend after the taping. . . ." Hayley said quietly.

"Hayley, no!" Liddy screamed, as Mona folded her arms, a self-satisfied smile on her face.

"It's just that I'm really nervous about tomorrow, and I need to get a good night's rest, and I'm fine if you want to go out on the town without me, but I have to prepare and think about how I'm going to present my bacon dish in under a minute in front of all those TV cameras and a full studio audience, and that's a lot of pressure, so I'd rather wait and have fun once it's all over."

More silence.

Although Mona's smile spoke volumes. She knew she had the vote in the bag.

The elevator doors opened on the thirty-eighth floor and Liddy shook her head before stepping off. "Fine. We'll stay in and order room service. But just tonight, do you hear me? I am not going to spend the entire weekend in the hotel because Mona doesn't want to pay for a club sandwich!"

After they trekked down the hall to their room and let themselves in using the card key, they found themselves in a deluxe room with two queen beds with swirly print bed wraps and white embroidered pillows set up against flat headboards that soared up to the ceiling.

Mona already had her hands on the TV remote and was jabbing at it with her index finger, trying to figure out all the functions.

Liddy raced into the bathroom to claim the majority of counter space and was calling back, "Bathroom's tiny for a five-star hotel, but I guess we can make do."

Hayley sat on the edge of one of the beds, which she was certain she would be sharing with Liddy since Mona was a restless sleeper and tossed and turned between her loud honking when she snored.

Both she and Liddy had picked up earplugs at the Bangor International Airport gift shop before the Bangor to Boston leg of their trip, knowing they would be sharing a room with Mona.

The butterflies in Hayley's stomach were already flapping so hard she had trouble catching her breath.

Liddy sailed out of the bathroom, feeling right at home in the plush accommodations, and noticed Hayley's pale face. She sat down beside Hayley on the bed.

"Honey, you're going to do a great job tomorrow. You have nothing to worry about," she said. "You're Hayley Powell, food-and-cocktails columnist for the *Island Times*! You're a star!"

Hayley smiled and rested her head on Liddy's shoulder. "Everybody at home is going to be watching and I just don't want to blow it."

Suddenly it sounded as if a man had burst into the room and was yelling at them, and they both jumped, but it was just Wolf Blitzer on *The Situation Room*.

Mona had found the volume button on the remote.

"Now it's after five, so we all know what that means," Liddy said.

They all responded in unison.

"Happy hour."

"Exactly," Liddy said, standing up and crossing to the desk to pick up the room service menu. "So let's calm our nerves with a cocktail since it seemed to do the trick on that horrific and traumatic flight here. We can also order some snacks and have a fun girls' night in a five-star hotel."

It sounded heavenly.

And it was.

At least it started out that way.

The freewheeling, loose slumber party began with a round of cosmos because that's what the girls on *Sex and the City* used to drink, according to Liddy. That led to a variety of martinis and a selection of entrées and appetizers from the room service menu, and before long they were cackling and gossiping, and Hayley was feeling much more relaxed and confident about the TV show taping tomorrow, and that's pretty much when the rest of the evening became a blur.

The next thing she knew she was lying on top of the bed wondering where she was as the sun streaked through a crack in the closed curtain and hit her directly in the face.

Hayley wrestled open a bloodshot eye and looked around.

The room was a mess.

Mona was face down on the floor and Liddy was a lump underneath the bed covers.

Or at least she hoped it was Liddy.

The floor was littered with empty food trays.

The minibar was ripped open and emptied.

It was like an all female version of that movie *The Hangover*.

At any moment, she expected a live goat to walk out of the bathroom.

She had no idea when the evening took such a wrong turn. Or what time it was.

Hell, she wasn't even sure what day it was.

And then it hit her so hard she was instantly clear eyed and sober.

It was Friday.

The day of *The Chat* taping.

She popped open her other eye and sat up on the bed, scanning the room for a clock.

She spotted one on the nightstand next to Liddy.

8:45 AM.

She was due to report to the set of the show at

8:30 AM for hair and makeup and pre-interview before the 10:00 AM live taping.

She was already fifteen minutes late.

"Liddy! Mona! Get up! We have to move now!"

She saw the lumpy figure underneath the bed wrap move slightly.

Mona was still passed out, her face hugging the rug, snoring.

Hayley leaped over Mona's body to get to the bathroom and frantically rummaged through her travel case for the eye cream she brought to treat the heavy dark bags underneath her eyes that were heightened now due to her partying the night before.

There was no time for a shower. She would just have to use extra deodorant.

Her hair was an unruly disaster and she prayed the professionals on call at the studio would be able to perform some kind of miracle.

She rummaged through her suitcase for the smart outfit she had chosen for her appearance. She had planned to iron it and make sure it didn't look bunched up and wrinkly.

No such luck.

She never got to it and when she pulled it out it looked as if she had slept in it all night.

There was no time to do anything about it.

She quickly dressed and shot out the door. Liddy and Mona would just have to fend for themselves and find their way to the taping if they were going to watch from the studio audience.

Hayley raced through the lobby and spotted one of the porters by the revolving glass door. "Taxi! I need a taxi!"

He looked a little scared as she ran toward him, eyes wild, hands in the air. He was probably debating whether to hail her a cab or run for his life.

Ever the professional, he scurried out the side door with a whistle and was flagging down a yellow cab as Hayley pushed through the revolving glass door so fast that she banged her shoulder taking too much time to step out into the street.

The porter had the door of a taxi cab open for her, and she practically did a swan dive into the back seat, reaching around to press a five-dollar bill into the porter's white-gloved hand.

"Thank you!" she screamed before turning her attention to a gruff-looking heavyset man behind the wheel smacking his gum and looking as if he'd rather be anywhere else.

"Where to?" he growled.

She had absolutely no idea.

She had left the detailed directions to the TV studio—so carefully printed out before the trip and placed in an envelope—on the desk in the hotel room.

There was no time to go back and get them. It was now past nine o'clock.

"I'm taping an episode of *The Chat* this morning!"

"Good for you," he said, unimpressed.

"Do you know it?"

"Yeah, it's that show with all those clucking women. I get that every night at the dinner table with my wife and her sister."

"Do you know where they tape it?"

"Yeah, actually their studio is—"

Hayley cut him off. "Take me there, please! Now!"

"But, lady . . ."

"I don't have time to talk! I need to get there right now!"

"I know, it's just—"

"Now! Now! Now!" she shrieked, pounding her fist on the glass divider that separated them and jolting him into action. As he swerved away from the curb and into passing traffic Hayley sat back, relieved she was finally on her way.

And then, after a few seconds, the car stopped again.

"What's going on? What are you doing? Why did we stop?"

He looked at her wearily through his rearview mirror. "We're here."

"What?"

Hayley looked out the window. The studio building was half a block from the hotel. If she had walked she would have gotten there faster.

The fare was a whopping two dollars and some change and that was mostly because it was the base fare.

She hurled a five at him through the divider and clamored out the door. "Thank you!"

She raced into the lobby where a harried production assistant was waiting for her. "We've been trying to call your cell for the last hour. What happened?"

Hayley had meant to charge it when she went to bed, but of course that never happened, because after all she hadn't even remembered to take off her clothes before going to bed, so the battery had probably died during the night.

"Never mind. There isn't any time to explain," the girl with thick black glasses and a T-shirt with *The Chat* logo on it said, as she ushered Hayley into an elevator and up to the eighth floor where she was then led into hair and makeup.

A very fabulous, very gay, very large black man with earrings and a purple blouse that flowed down his ample belly like a caftan grabbed her by the arm and forced her down in a chair.

He took one look at her hair and shook his head. "Girl, you got hair going in every direction. It's like a large crowd running out of a burning building! Not to worry. Calvin's got you covered."

He made her feel slightly more relaxed. She turned to the production assistant. "Do you have an iron? I'd like to smooth out my shirt and pants before the taping if there's time."

"I'm sure we can find you one," the production assistant said, before glancing up from her clipboard. "Now, did you bring the ingredients for your bacon dish?"

Hayley's mouth dropped open.

She hadn't brought any ingredients.

She had submitted her recipe via e-mail to the show's producers, but no one had said anything about providing her own ingredients.

She was about to go before a national television audience and prepare Bacon-Wrapped Jalapeño-Stuffed Chicken Thighs with no bacon, no chicken, and no jalapeño to stuff it with.

This did not bode well for her first TV appearance.

Chapter 5

After a hair and makeup session that was as speedy as a NASCAR racing pit crew changing a tire, Hayley was bundled into a silk robe and quickly ushered down a hall to a door while her shirt was being pressed.

The panicked production assistant lightly tapped on it.

There was a growl from inside. "Come in!"

The assistant turned to Hayley and forced a slight smile before gently opening the door.

A loud booming voice was in the middle of a tirade. "I'm not just going to sit here and take this! If you people can't do anything about it, then I will!"

It was Rhonda Franklin.

Hayley's whole body shrunk from fright.

She had read the gossip pages.

Temper tantrums on the set.

Twitter feuds.

Scathing op-ed pieces excoriating any public political figure who disagreed with her very strong, strident views.

Rhonda Franklin did not suffer fools lightly.

And right now Hayley was the biggest fool in the building for daring to show up to prepare a bacon dish with no ingredients.

Hayley jumped as she heard something smash against the wall inside the dressing room.

She pictured Rhonda hurling her phone across the room.

"Don't hover outside! I hate people who hover! Get the hell in here already!" Rhonda bellowed.

The production assistant grabbed a fistful of Hayley's silk robe and gave her a strong shove into the dressing room.

Rhonda was in an orange pantsuit, her dark brown hair in curlers, and her face caked in makeup. Her frame was large and imposing and her piercing green eyes stared at the shaking production assistant with a laserlike focus. "Whose brilliant idea was it to put me in this orange pantsuit? I look like a mutated pumpkin!"

"I'm sorry, Rhonda, I don't know who—"

"Well, find out, and when you do send him or her to my dressing room! Now!"

The production assistant nodded vigorously and skedaddled, leaving Hayley to face the TV host's wrath alone with no obvious means of defense.

It took Rhonda a few seconds to realize there was someone still in the room. "Who the hell are you?"

"I'm . . . I'm . . ." Hayley couldn't remember her own name. "I'm on the show today . . . making bacon. . . ."

What the hell was she making?

Her mind was a blank.

Rhonda was unamused.

"Bacon-wrapped Hayley . . . I mean jalapeño. . . ."

Rhonda suddenly brightened. "Stuffed Chicken Thighs? Oh my God, is it you? Are you Hayley Powell?"

Hayley managed a nod and a half smile.

"I saw the show notes! That's one of your best recipes ever! I can't believe I'm finally meeting you! I'm a huge fan!" Rhonda squealed, her arms outstretched as she lumbered over and grabbed her in a tight hug.

Hayley felt as if her bones were cracking and she couldn't breathe.

But the pain was nothing compared to just a few seconds earlier when she imagined Rhonda was going to physically pick her up and hurl her out of the dressing room.

"I was so excited when I heard you had agreed to be on the show! I never miss your column! You crack me up with your stories! What a hoot! I have to say—"

A man's voice interrupted her.

"Excuse me, Rhonda. I just wanted to drop by to say a quick hello before we go on the air. . . ."

Rhonda's megawatt smile dimmed slightly and she rolled her eyes, annoyed as she did a quick half turn toward the door. "Okay, Bradley, see you out there."

Hayley glanced at the gentleman standing in the door frame.

Tall, gorgeous, with curly brown hair.

His handsome face was very familiar.

Bradley lingered a few seconds longer, but Rhonda had already turned back to Hayley. "Do you know I had never even heard of a Lemon Drop Martini before you wrote about it?"

Bradley shrugged and walked away.

And that's it dawned on Hayley. "Was that Bradley—?"

"Cooper. Yeah. He's on the show today," Rhonda said, before leaning in and winking at Hayley. "Between you and me, he's a bit needy."

Hayley's knees buckled.

She had just been in the same room with Bradley Cooper.

"Look, I want to show you," Rhonda said, taking Hayley by the hand and leading her over to a small cupboard, which she opened to reveal a fully stocked bar. Prominently displayed in the front were the necessary ingredients for Hayley's Lemon Drop Martini. "I figured we can have one after the taping!"

Hayley was overwhelmed by Rhonda's charm and effusive personality. She was so different from the angry, intimidating Rhonda who was bellowing when she'd first entered the room.

Hayley caught the time on a Mickey Mouse clock hanging on the dressing room wall.

9:50 AM.

The taping was scheduled to begin in ten minutes.

She had to tell someone she didn't have the ingredients for her recipe.

She took a deep breath and blurted out, "Rhonda, I forgot to bring the ingredients for my bacon recipe and I don't know what to do."

She closed her eyes, expecting the first, less friendly Rhonda to come charging back.

But she didn't.

Without missing a beat, Rhonda said softly, "Do you have a list?"

She did.

In the front pocket of her slacks, which were at this moment being ironed.

She had put it there last night before her cocktail hour (or hours) with Liddy and Mona for safekeeping because she knew she would be wearing those pants to the TV taping.

She told Rhonda where her list was.

"Lily! Get in here!" Rhonda shouted.

A preppy redheaded girl in a stylish top and designer jeans and wearing red-tinted wire-rim glasses suddenly appeared through a side door that connected to another room.

"There's a piece of paper in Hayley's pants that are being pressed right now. Go get it and hightail it over to the Whole Foods around the corner. Buy everything on that list and be back in ten minutes!"

"Right!"

She flew out the door.

With a smile, Rhonda turned back to Hayley. "That's Lily, my personal assistant. She's so much more reliable than any of the idiot hipsters they got working on this show. Most are here because they're the lazy spawn of some network executive or corporate sponsor. Lily's different. She's worked hard to get here."

Hayley still couldn't believe all this was happening.

She was in New York.

Hanging with Rhonda Franklin in her dressing room.

And they had just blown off Bradley Cooper.

It was like a dream.

She was jolted back to reality by something crawling up her leg.

Startled, Hayley looked down to see a potbellied pig at her feet, his snout up underneath her robe, sniffing and snorting.

Hayley jumped.

Rhonda clapped her hands. "Pork Chop!" She bent down to pet the little pig.

Hayley was impressed by Rhonda's limber move given the bulk of her body.

Rhonda lifted the pig and he nuzzled her ample breast. "How are you doing, my little piggly wiggly?"

"There he is! He's always breaking free to explore!"

A statuesque woman in a bar-code-print paneled silk dress with a feathery hat and dark sunglasses swept into the now crowded dressing room. She picked up the leash that was attached to a diamond-studded collar the pig had around his neck that was probably worth more than Hayley made in a year.

"I hope he hasn't been bothering you," the woman purred.

"You know I love this pig!" Rhonda cooed, planting five kisses on top of the pig's head. "Olivia, this is Hayley Powell, the chef I've been raving about."

"Chef" was a fancier title than Hayley deserved. She just experimented in her kitchen on occasion and wrote about it.

"A pleasure, Hayley," Olivia said, holding out her hand, waiting for Hayley to take it. She quickly obliged and the woman continued. "I never miss reading your column when I'm visiting the island."

Hayley knew exactly who this woman was.

Olivia Redmond.

Heiress to Redmond Meats, the leading supplier of meat products in the country, if not the world, with a specific emphasis on bacon, their top seller. The family owned a sprawling estate on Mount Desert Island, which they opened to the public every Fourth of July for a catered barbecue that employed almost as many locals as the ones who attended as guests.

Olivia's father had passed away after a long illness not too long ago and she was left pretty much the whole enchilada, and was installed as the company's new CEO. The *Island Times* did a story on how there was a lot of company infighting over Olivia taking over, but Olivia's father had enlisted an army of lawyers before his death to insure his only living child became the sole heir and dominant shareholder, so there was very little the Board of Directors could do to stop it.

Rhonda gave Olivia a light kiss on the cheek and handed Pork Chop back to his mommy. "So glad you could make it. How could we do a Salute to Bacon without you?"

"Well, we're running three ads during the show, so I'm sure the audience will be sick of hearing about Redmond Meats by the time I show my face in the fourth segment," Olivia said.

"Darling, you're needed in makeup," a heavily accented man's voice said.

Hayley's heart skipped a beat at the sight of the bronze-skinned Adonis in the doorway, whose muscled arm flexed when he reached out to touch Olivia on the arm. He was in a tight-fitting polo shirt and crisp dark slacks. He had dreamy brown eyes and matching curly hair and his voice was deep and melodious.

This had to be Nacho.

Olivia's famous polo-playing Argentinean husband.

Olivia had first spotted him modeling in a two-page cologne ad in *Vanity Fair* magazine and just had to have him.

And she got him.

In record time.

The world's dreamiest trophy husband.

"I better go. The makeup folks are going to need as much time as they can get to fix this," Olivia said, her face flawless and wrinkle free even though she was in her mid to late forties.

"Get out of here! You're beautiful!" Rhonda yelled, smiling.

Nacho put a hand on the small of her back to lead her out.

Hayley sighed when he turned to go. His butt was perfection. Like a Greek statue at a museum.

The next hour was a blur. Much like the night before with Liddy and Mona in the hotel room.

The pretty personal assistant, Lily, returned with a bag full of food and Hayley was escorted to a private kitchen away from the set where she was able to marinate her chicken thighs. Usually she preferred to allow the thighs to marinate overnight, but she was in a time crunch and her segment was set to begin at 10:45. She heard wild applause in the distance as the show's hosts were introduced and the show got under way.

The first production assistant returned with Hayley's

blouse and slacks, which were freshly pressed and scented. Then she was whisked back to makeup and hair for a final touch-up, where a flat screen TV on the wall allowed her to watch the ladies gush over Bradley Cooper, whom they were interviewing.

Once they finished with Bradley, Olivia was brought on with her potbellied pig, Pork Chop, with whom the audience instantly fell in love. Olivia talked about Bacon Week and how her favorite meat had always gotten a bad wrap. Hayley didn't see the rest of the segment because she was whisked backstage with two other chefs who looked equally nervous.

Hayley was placed behind a small cooking station with all her ingredients and plates and utensils. The hot lights started to slowly melt the caked gunk on her face and she feared her mascara would smear and make her look like a raccoon on national TV. But there was no time to worry because suddenly Rhonda closed in and, holding a microphone in front of her face, asked her about what she was going to prepare today.

Hayley had no idea what was happening. She had no clue what she said as she rolled chicken thighs up to stuff cheese and jalapeño peppers inside before wrapping bacon strips around the thighs and securing them with toothpicks. She was surprised when Rhonda opened an oven door and pulled out the finished dish and then picked up a nearby fork to taste it. A staffer must have pre-prepared the recipe so they could try some on the show. Hayley hadn't even thought of that.

Rhonda moaned in ecstasy and rubbed her belly and then put an arm around Hayley and shoved the microphone in her face one more time. Again, Hayley had no clue what Rhonda asked or how she responded.

The audience erupted in applause, and that's when Hayley caught a glimpse of Liddy and Mona in the front row of the bleachers, on their feet, spastically clapping their hands and whooping and hollering.

Then the red light on the camera flicked off and everyone moved back to the main set for the show's wrap-up.

Hayley closed her eyes.

A magnificent sense of relief washed over her.

It was over.

Island Food & Spirits
by
Hayley Powell

After an exciting few days in the Big Apple, I think I'm finally coming back to earth and reality.

My e-mail in-box has been flooded with requests for the recipe that I prepared on the show, so today I would love to share it with you.

I've been kid free lately, so I invited my brother, Randy, and his husband, Sergio, over for dinner the night after I returned home from New York to try one of my favorite new cocktails, a Mexican Martini, before serving my now famous (at least in local circles) spicy Bacon-Wrapped Jalapeño-Stuffed Chicken Thighs.

Dinner was delicious, and the cocktails were flowing when my brother remarked that it was amazing how much I love bacon (I eat it almost every day, cholesterol be damned!), especially after the incident early on in my marriage to my ex-husband, Danny.

The story Randy was referring to happened just after Danny and I tied the knot and rented a tiny one-bedroom house on Crooked Road with an equally tiny backyard.

Like most newlyweds, we were on a very tight budget and always trying to save money anywhere we could, so for our eggs and bacon we would run up the road to the Jones Family Farm on Saturday mornings and load up on fresh eggs and bacon at a low price that fed us for a whole week!

One Saturday, Danny left to pick up our eggs and bacon and was gone for almost an hour. I started to worry, and was about to call Mr. Jones to see if he was still there, when Danny pulled up in his truck. I heard him burst through the back door to the kitchen and went to meet him to make sure he stored the eggs and bacon in the refrigerator. (He sometimes was easily distracted, once leaving an unopened carton of ice cream on the counter to melt into mush.)

As I met him in the kitchen, the first words out of my mouth were, "What in the world have you done, and where's my bacon?"

Danny just stood there in the middle of our tiny kitchen, a big dumb smile on his face and a tiny bundle in his arms wrapped in a dish towel. He unwrapped the towel to reveal a baby piglet.

My gut told me to take the piglet back to the Jones farm immediately, but I'm a sucker for a cute animal, so I was instantly smitten. I never even heard Danny say, "This will save us a ton of money. We can raise him and then he can provide us this coming winter's bacon and pork supply."

Apparently his words were drowned out by my cooing as I cuddled the adorable piglet in my arms and whispered in his tiny ear, "I'm naming you Bubba."

Well, it wasn't long before Bubba was eating us right out of house and home and costing us our hard-earned savings, which was a pittance to begin with since I was pregnant with my daughter, Gemma, and not working.

Within a week, Bubba rooted and ate our entire vegetable garden, destroyed every inch of our backyard (which emptied out our already small savings account). We tried satisfying Bubba's huge appetite with grain from the feed store and any leftovers that we had begged and hoarded from our neighbors and friends.

Even though Bubba was high maintenance, I still loved the little pig.

Except he wasn't so little.

After eight weeks, he was already a whopping sixty pounds.

Whenever Bubba's antics stressed me out, Danny would pipe up and re-assure me that it would all be over in a few months and we would be chowing down like kings during the cold winter months!

Again, I'm not really sure why I didn't hear this.

By the time Bubba was six months old, he was a jaw dropping 280 pounds! And he was no longer popular with the neighbors. He had broken through our little wooden fence, trampling and eating Mrs. Gray's entire prize flower garden. He terrorized some neighbor children who were having their first campout alone in their backyard when he broke down the fence and began rooting around their tent for food, all the while snorting and grunting. The poor kids' terrified screams about a hideous monster lurking about had every neighbor with a shotgun (which on the island is just about everyone) running around the street and into the woods in search of the Bigfoot-like mythical creature. Luckily we man-aged to lure Bubba home with some celery sticks until things settled down.

His rampage continued into late

fall. He ate another neighbor's fresh fruit and veggies she had bought at the farmers' market when she left them on her steps while carrying her other groceries into her house. And what was almost the last straw, the police showed up in our neighborhood because some tourists riding their bikes called 911 to report being attacked by a wild boar.

In Bubba's defense, he was just saying hello. He was a very friendly pig. But his presence was a toll on our neighbors and our now overdrawn bank account.

Finally, the day came when it was time for Bubba to—how can I say it?—pay us back.

On the day Danny loaded him into a borrowed trailer and headed out, it dawned on me that my big sweet boy was about to become a pile of bacon.

I cried and swore I wouldn't eat a piece of bacon ever again! Especially not my Bubba! I would become a vegan! Yes, I was that distraught.

When Danny returned home, I couldn't even go to greet him. I was curled up on the couch, a blanket wrapped around me, a complete blubbering mess. He handed me a package of store-bought bacon for our winter freezer and an envelope stuffed with money.

"Where did you get this?" I asked, sniffing.

"Pig farm outside Belfast. The owner thought Bubba was a nice, good-looking, unusually large pig, so he bought him to be a breeder pig so he can sire a whole bunch of giant pigs!"

Bubba had been given a reprieve!

He was no longer on death row!

And I was still able to eat bacon.

I just stopped thinking about where it came from.

One way to do that is to have a strong Mexican Martini designed to help you forget just about everything.

Mexican Martini

Ingredients
1 ounce blue curaçao
1 ounce your favorite tequila
½ ounce Midori melon liquor
½ ounce triple sec
Favorite fruit to garnish (optional)

Add ice to a shaker, then pour all of the ingredients. Shake and strain into a chilled martini glass. Garnish if you wish, then be prepared to be wowed.

Bacon-Wrapped Jalapeño-Stuffed Chicken Thighs

<u>Ingredients</u>

Package of boneless, skinless chicken
    thighs
1 8-ounce package pepper-jack
    cheese
1 small jar sliced jalapeños
1 package thick-sliced bacon
1 bottle mesquite (or your favorite
    flavor)
Toothpicks

Marinate the chicken thighs in your favorite marinade flavor for at least 45 minutes or even overnight for more flavor. Slice the cheese into ⅛-inch slices. Remove two jalapeños per chicken thigh from the jar and set aside on paper towel. Place one piece of bacon per chicken thigh on a plate.

To assemble, lay a chicken thigh on a piece of bacon. Put a slice of cheese on the thigh, followed by two jalapeño slices on top of cheese. Roll chicken thigh up so the cheese and jalapeño are stuffed inside. Then wrap the bacon strip around the thigh and secure with toothpicks.

Repeat until all the thighs are done. Grill for about 25 minutes and enjoy!

Chapter 6

Never in her wildest dreams had Hayley ever believed she would finally have a better understanding of what poor Taylor Swift went through.

The plugged in pop star was world famous and dogged by adoring fans wherever she went. And now, after just swinging into the Shop 'n Save to buy a bag of frozen stir-fry vegetables she had planned on heating up in the wok with a handful of peanuts and some soy sauce for her dinner, Hayley was surrounded by a gaggle of excited high school girls who were jostling to get a selfie for their Instagram pages.

"Hayley, look this way!" one snaggletoothed, mop-topped girl squealed before shoving her phone in front of Hayley's face and blinding her with a sudden flash.

The girls actually knew her name.

She wasn't just "Dustin's mother."

Shoppers had to take a detour around them with their carts because they were clogging the aisle.

"My mom's making your Bacon-Wrapped Jalapeño-Stuffed Chicken Thighs recipe for dinner tonight!" another girl said before hooking an arm around Hayley's neck and smiling brightly as she snapped a photo with her own phone.

Hayley was disoriented from all the flashes and felt as if she was being tossed around like a rag doll as the girls took turns snapping pictures. Finally, after one big group photo taken by a stock boy with a stupid grin on his face, who was willing to do just about anything the cute older high school girls asked of him, Hayley was allowed to continue her grocery shopping.

After hunting down the few items she needed, she made a beeline for the checkout line. She spent another ten minutes nodding and thanking locals who were checking out at the same time as they complimented her appearance on *The Chat*. She patiently answered their burning questions about the stars of the show, especially Rhonda Franklin, whom a few of them had spotted tooling around the island in recent years.

The cashier who began scanning Hayley's items had worked at the store for years and had barely managed a smile whenever Hayley checked out at her register. But today she was beaming from ear to ear, adjusting her glasses to get a better look at what Hayley was wearing, and was uncharacteristically warm and polite.

This was all too much.

Hayley just wanted to get to her car and finally have some peace.

She had never expected this kind of reaction when

she and Liddy and Mona touched down at Bangor International Airport the night before. By then the episode had aired and it was now the only thing everyone in town could talk about.

Hayley would be lying if she said she didn't enjoy the attention just a tiny bit, but enough was enough, and she was anxious for her life to get back to normal.

Her one previous brush with fame was appearing on a coupon-clipping game show a few years back, but that was on an obscure cable network that half the town didn't even have on their channel lineup. This was a major broadcast network, and not only that, Hayley's short clip from the show was all over the Internet. Her little stint as Rachael Ray for a day was everywhere.

Hayley mercifully made it to her car, dropped the recyclable bag with her groceries in the passenger seat, and returned to the office to put in her last few hours before she could go home for the day.

When she arrived, she stored her dinner in the refrigerator located in the back bull pen and returned to her desk to check her e-mails.

It was quiet. All of the paper's reporters were out in the field. The office was empty.

But then she heard a hissing sound.

She worried the refrigerator was on the fritz again and her frozen vegetables would thaw.

The hissing stopped and was followed by a groan and then steady wheezing.

Sal was napping at his desk.

A typical occurrence after he returned from a long bourbon-fueled lunch with his fishing buddies.

Good for Sal. He was having trouble sleeping at night lately, so it was important he get a little shut-eye during the day to make up for it.

Suddenly the door to the front office flew open and banged loudly as Bruce stormed in, a rolled up newspaper squeezed inside his fist.

She heard a loud grunt in the back. The noise had startled Sal awake.

So much for his much needed rest.

"Everything all right, Bruce?"

Bruce stopped and glared at Hayley. "I suppose you've seen the front page of today's paper."

"Actually, it's been a little crazy around here today and I haven't had the chance."

Bruce unfurled the paper to reveal a front page photo of Hayley next to Rhonda Franklin while she was stuffing one of Hayley's chicken thighs in her mouth on the set of *The Chat*. The picture took up half the front page and the headline plastered over the top read, LOCAL CHEF HEATS UP CHAT SHOW.

"Chef? Sal called me a chef?" Hayley asked, unable to suppress a smile.

Studying the picture, she was, surprisingly, quite pleased at what she saw.

She didn't look half bad.

Hayley had previously thought it was impossible for her to take a decent photo. Her eyes were usually closed or her hair was too frizzy or her smile was crooked.

But there she was on the front page of the *Island Times* looking, dare she say it, not unattractive.

"Yes, the shot is adorable and you look about as cute and lovable as a beagle chasing a tennis ball, but this whole issue is crap! Let me be the first one to tell you, Hayley! This paper is on a major downward spiral!"

Hayley thought it wise to warn Bruce that Sal was in the back, but he didn't give her a chance.

"It's been a slow decline! It started with Sal emphasizing human interest pieces to sell more papers! Maybe one or two a week. But now it's an epidemic! It's every day! You fly to New York to feed an overweight has-been actress trying to save her career with a morning talk show and you make the front page! I do an exhaustive, hard-hitting investigation on the disappearance of a major medical researcher, Dr. Alvin Foley, whose disappearance may have global implications, and I'm relegated to page four! Page four! Honestly, Hayley, I can't take it anymore! I'm ready to—"

"Quit?"

"No! Give Sal a piece of my mind!"

"Well, congratulations, Bruce, you can mark that off your check list."

"Why? What do you mean?"

Her eyes moved behind Bruce to the open door to the bull pen where Sal stood, fuming, the blood vessels in his face ready to burst.

Bruce's own face suddenly went pale and his entire body sagged.

He slowly turned around and said in a meek, barely audible voice, "Sal, I thought you were still at lunch."

"You listen to me, Brucie," Sal said, his voice a low growl. "Maybe if you had come up with one shred of evidence, anything that might explain what happened to Dr. Foley, then I would slap it on page one. But you haven't written anything newsworthy since the guy just up and vanished. Nothing! So until you stop pontificating and indulging yourself like some armchair detective with ridiculous speculative theories about what *you think* may have happened to him and start focusing on hard facts, your column's going to remain in the back pages, are we clear?"

"Yes, Sal," Bruce whispered, sweat pouring down his face.

"Now, if you'll excuse me, I heard Sally Jenkins's Maine coon cat is about to have a litter of kittens, so I'm meeting a photographer over at her house to take some pictures and do a story for tomorrow's front page," Sal said, barreling past Bruce for the door.

"Are you serious?"

"No, I'm not serious, you imbecile! I'm going to Drinks Like A Fish for a bourbon! I'm too pissed to hang around here anymore!"

Sal charged out, making sure to slam the door behind him.

Bruce cleared his throat, pretended he wasn't dying inside, and slinked into the back bull pen.

Hayley sighed.

Just another day at the office.

Chapter 7

Why hadn't Hayley listened to the little voice inside her head that was telling her to go straight home after work?

She would have saved herself a world of humiliation.

But no.

She had to drive over to Aaron's office on a whim just to check in and say hello. They hadn't spoken all week and she wanted to see for herself if he was upset with her or if his feelings for her had cooled.

Actually, deep down she was hoping she would be greeted by that warm, inviting smile and the ever present twinkle in his eye when he saw her in his waiting room.

Hopefully all of her concerns and fears that something had changed in their relationship would finally be put to rest for good.

No such luck.

He rushed out from the back after being summoned by his new receptionist, an older, dour woman with a severe tone whom he had hired after Gemma left for college. Her name was Edna and she was retired but enjoyed the part-time work. Or at least she said she enjoyed it. You couldn't tell from her expression because she never cracked a smile.

Aaron was in a blue dress shirt that was wrinkled. The sleeves were rolled up and his red tie was askew. He looked tired and haggard; his hair was mussed and his face drawn. "Hayley, what's wrong? Why are you here?"

Not the words she wanted to be greeted with, but it was too late to turn around and get the hell out of there. She had stepped in it and there was no turning back.

"I . . . I just was curious to see how you're doing. We haven't spoken in a while."

Oh, God, why did she say that last part?

Now she was coming across as the needy girlfriend.

He gestured to the five pet owners seated quietly in chairs behind her, two with dogs, one with a cat, one with a caged parakeet, and then there was the young boy holding a glass case in his lap with what looked like a giant snake inside curled up and still.

"As you can see, it's kind of crazy around here today. I'm sorry. Can I call you later?"

"Of course. I didn't mean to bother you. . . . I'm so sorry."

He smiled. "I miss you. Let me call you later and we'll plan something for this weekend, okay?"

"Yes. I'm sorry."

"Stop apologizing. You've done nothing wrong. I'm glad you stopped by. I just have to get back to a cocker spaniel with an eye infection."

"Yes, yes, go! We'll talk later."

He nodded, taking one last look at her to make sure she wasn't upset, and then whipped around and raced back to his exam room.

Edna looked up from her computer, her reading glasses perched on the edge of her nose, her face full of judgment. She glared at Hayley as if she was an unwanted intruder.

And in a way, she was.

Suddenly she felt a familiar wet nose snorting her pant leg.

She looked down to see Pork Chop, the potbellied pig, curiously smelling her. He was pulled back by a yank on that astoundingly expensive diamond-collared leash he wore around his neck by Olivia Redmond.

"Stop bothering the poor lady, Pork Chop."

"Ms. Redmond, you're here early this year, aren't you? You usually don't arrive until the weather gets better in June," Hayley said, bending down and petting Pork Chop on the head.

"I needed to get away, so I had the staff open the house early this year. I arrived this morning. Pork Chop is due for a couple of shots."

"Do you have an appointment?" Edna asked, already knowing the answer since her eyes were glued to the calendar on her computer.

"No, I don't," Olivia said, brushing past Hayley and staring down at the crotchety old woman who was throwing her attitude. "But I'm sure Dr. Palmer will see me first chance he gets. You're new here, so you probably don't realize I don't need to make an appointment. Olivia Redmond."

Hayley dreamed of having the confidence of

someone who is accustomed to getting whatever she damn well pleases.

Edna picked up the phone and punched in an extension, all the while never taking her eyes off Olivia. She raised a bony hand to cover her mouth as she whispered into the receiver, and after a few moments her angry face melted away and was replaced by a flicker of worry, and then a forced smile as she put the phone down.

"Please have a seat, Ms. Redmond. Dr. Palmer will be with you shortly."

"Thank you," Olivia said, turning her back on Edna and rolling her eyes at Hayley, who tried not to snicker.

"Is there anything else I can help you with, Hayley?"

"No, I was just leaving," Hayley said, copying Olivia by dramatically turning her back on Edna, but she just didn't have the gravitas or class to carry it off like Olivia had just done.

"It was so nice seeing you again," Hayley said to Olivia, who had just plopped down on the last remaining chair and was holding Pork Chop in her lap while gently stroking his head.

"Yes, a pleasure. Are you free for dinner tomorrow night?"

Hayley sputtered, "Tomorrow, why, yes, I'm sure I'm free."

"Good. You can join me and my husband at the Blooming Rose. I've heard great things about the food and have been dying to try it. It would be a real treat for us to dine with a professional chef and get your honest opinion."

"Oh, I'm not—" Hayley stopped herself. She had

promised not to shy away from anyone calling her a chef anymore.

Why put herself down like that? She had a regular column with kitchen-tested recipes, so why not own it?

She was a chef.

And she wasn't about to correct a billion-dollar heiress who at this very moment was calling her one. "I would be honored to join you for dinner, Ms. Redmond."

"Olivia, please. We're friends now. I'll make a reservation and e-mail you tomorrow with a time."

"I'm looking forward to it," Hayley said, glancing back at Edna, whose mouth was so far open Hayley resisted the temptation to warn her against catching flies.

Instead, she held her head high and breezed out the door.

She no longer felt humiliated for barging in on Aaron. She felt vindicated and in high spirits.

If only this elated feeling would last.

Little did she know it was all about to come crashing down in a big way.

Chapter 8

"The seafood tastes funny," Olivia said, practically gagging as she spit out what was in her mouth into a yellow cloth napkin and rolled it up into a ball.

She had ordered the Salmon-Stuffed Maine Crab Cakes with a spicy wasabi sauce off the menu, and when it arrived Hayley thought it looked absolutely delicious.

Olivia's handsome, suave husband, Nacho, kept his eyes glued to his plate and picked at his pan-seared halibut, fearing what was about to come.

Hayley simply tried to diffuse the situation by popping a gnocchi slathered in a brown-butter-sage sauce into her own mouth and moaning. "Mine is so good. The sauce is just bursting with flavor. And those fried raviolis with the basil and tomato marinara dipping sauce I had for an appetizer were incredible."

It wasn't enough to stop Olivia from cranking her head around in search of the willowy young hostess in the pink sundress. "Excuse me, young lady, I'd like to speak to the owner."

The girl nodded, her face a frozen mask of dread, and then she disappeared into the kitchen.

"I expected more of this place," Olivia said, slamming her fork down and then picking up a glass of ice water and gulping it.

A restaurant with an impeccable reputation, the Blooming Rose was situated on the outskirts of the tiny hamlet of Town Hill in a small New England cottage nestled in a wooded area. It was a fifteen-minute drive from the center of Bar Harbor but always worth it for its culinary treats for the taste buds.

Hayley was thrilled because she had been dying to try it ever since they opened early for the season, a full six weeks ahead of their usual date, which was around Memorial Day.

The meal started out innocently enough with an array of appetizers, including the fried raviolis along with a local artisan cheese plate and a chilled lobster salad with a tarragon vinaigrette.

In fact, Hayley was in absolute heaven.

She made a note to write about this flawless meal in a future column, not only to praise the delicious food but also because she was fond of the owner, Felicity Flynn-Chan, who was always so kind to Hayley when she called the paper to place ads for the restaurant.

But then came the entrées, and although Hayley and Nacho were both pleased with their selections, she quickly noticed an appalled look of distaste suddenly appear on Olivia's face, and her mood instantly darkened.

She didn't like her seafood.

And it was going to be a big problem.

Felicity entered the dining room from the kitchen and bravely crossed to their table, a tight smile fixed on her face. "Ivy tells me you wanted to see me."

"Yes," Olivia said, turning her head and speaking in the most haughty, snobbish manner she could muster. "My name is Olivia Redmond. . . ."

"Yes, Ms. Redmond, of course I know you—"

"Please allow me to finish," Olivia barked.

Felicity clammed up.

"I visit the island every summer and dine at all the restaurants in town, and I was so much looking forward to enjoying a meal here since all my friends seem to rave about this place, but I can't eat these crab cakes. They're too fishy and too spicy!"

Hayley wanted to shrink in her seat, but Felicity remained calm and collected and reached down to pick up the plate of half-eaten crab cakes in front of Olivia. "Then please, let me bring you something else."

Olivia slapped her hand away. "I don't want anything else. This rotten fish has ruined my palette."

"I assure you, Ms. Redmond, the salmon in the crab cakes is fresh."

"It damn well may be, but it tastes lousy. You should consider investing in a new chef because whatever he's done to these crab cakes is a culinary crime."

"My sweet potato gnocchi is delicious," Hayley said impulsively, stabbing three pieces of gnocchi on her fork and shoveling it into her mouth. "Can't get enough of it."

Felicity offered her a slight but grateful smile.

Olivia chose to ignore her.

Felicity sighed. She was adhering to the rule that the customer was always right, but it was a downright challenge. "My husband, Alan, is our chef. He prepared the crab cakes. I'm sorry it's not to your liking, but he has been trained all over Europe and Asia, and very rarely do we ever hear complaints about his talents."

"I'm sure your husband, Alan, has an illustrious career ahead of him in the fast-food industry," Olivia said, pushing her chair back. "I've had enough of your back talk. Clearly you are uninterested in my opinion."

"On the contrary, I take what you're saying very seriously. . . ."

"Not seriously enough, I'm afraid. The chef is still in the kitchen working. Let's go. I'm sure I can find something edible at home."

Olivia swiveled around to make sure her back was to Felicity as she stormed out. "Pay the bill, Nacho."

Nacho reached for his wallet but Felicity stopped him.

"Please, the least I can do is comp the meal," Felicity said, sighing.

Hayley glimpsed Felicity's good-looking, slight, wiry husband, Alan, poking his head above the carved wood swinging doors leading into the kitchen to see what was happening.

When he saw Hayley staring at him, he panicked and disappeared back inside. She had only met him once, at a wine-tasting party in town, and found him soft-spoken but warm and charming.

Felicity was the one in charge and running the show.

And everyone in town knew it.

But that didn't seem to bother him. He probably married her because he liked a strong woman telling him what to do.

"I'm sure part of the reason she's being so difficult is because you refused to allow her to bring her pig in here to dine on scraps underneath the table," Nacho said, shaking his head.

"It's the law, I'm sorry," Felicity said, shrugging her shoulders.

"Again, I *loved* my meal," Hayley said as she stood up from the table, having polished off most of it. "I only wish we could stay for dessert."

"Next time," Felicity said, smiling.

"Thank you for your kindness," Nacho said, shaking Felicity's hand before rushing out to calm his irritable wife.

Hayley turned to Felicity. "I am so embarrassed."

"Don't be," Felicity said. "I have to handle impossible customers all the time. It's really no big deal. In fact, most of them usually come back later in the summer and are very well behaved. Mostly because all their friends have talked up the place and they don't want to feel like they're missing out on something."

"Well, it's nice to see you take it all in stride."

"Part of the job," Felicity said.

Hayley couldn't resist picking up her fork and trying the crab cake. She chewed it for a few seconds, the taste exploding in her mouth. "Oh my God, this is scrumptious. How could she complain about it?"

"Like her husband suggested, her churlish behavior had very little to do with not liking the food," Felicity said.

"Would you mind . . . ?"

"Of course. Let me get you a doggy bag," Felicity said, reading her mind.

"Make sure it's big enough to fit Nacho's halibut. I'd hate to see that go to waste too," Hayley said.

Felicity gave her a wink and breezed into the kitchen.

After stocking up on the leftovers, which she was sure would be consumed before bedtime, Hayley carried the brown paper bag out to the gravel-lined parking lot to her Kia. She spotted Olivia's Rolls Royce still parked in a spot underneath a leafy tree on the far end of the lot, closest to the woods. She saw Nacho walking Pork Chop on that sparkling diamond-studded leash down a path, probably so he could take care of business before the ride back to the Redmond Estate.

The back door to the rolls opened and Olivia got out and waved at Hayley. "I need to speak to you before you leave," she yelled, startling her.

Hayley nodded, dreading what was about to come, and then casually hid the doggie bag behind her as she slowly and deliberately walked over to the silver Rolls. "Yes?"

"I meant to discuss this with you at dinner, but that was before it all went so horribly wrong and I didn't get the chance. I couldn't stay there a moment longer."

"What is it, Olivia?" Hayley said, praying she wouldn't smell the contents in the brown paper bag she clutched in her hand behind her left leg.

"I've been speaking to the administrator of our Redmond Meats Web site and we've decided we need a cooking blog, someone to post bacon-flavored recipes once or twice a week, and I was wondering if you . . ."

"I'm sure I could come up with a few names."

"No, Hayley, I want *you*. Now, I know you have your column with the paper, but I promise you it won't interfere, and if your editor has a problem with you moonlighting, I would be happy to speak to him about it. The paper will always come first."

Hayley was floored.

"I respect your skills, Hayley. Rhonda was kind enough to allow me to try that yummy chicken recipe you shared on her show and I was duly impressed. Plus you're a local, which adds to your charm. We love the Redmond connection to Maine and want to promote that on the site."

"I don't know what to say. . . ."

"Say yes. I'll pay you well. Two hundred a column."

Two hundred bucks a couple of times a week?

That was all she needed to hear.

"Of course. Thank you."

Olivia hugged her, squeezing her tightly for a few seconds, and then abruptly pulled away. That was probably about as much as she could endure in the affection department.

"I'll call you tomorrow," Olivia purred before climbing back into the Rolls and shutting the door.

Nacho hurried up the path with Pork Chop, who scampered at his side, and they hopped in the other side.

The driver pulled away, leaving Hayley alone with her bag of leftover gourmet food.

She knew she had done the right thing jumping at this rare opportunity. How could she not for at least four hundred extra dollars a week?

But having witnessed the mercurial side of Olivia Redmond inside the Blooming Rose restaurant, there was a tiny voice inside her screaming that she was asking for big time trouble.

And you know what they say about those voices.

If the voice is loud enough, you should probably listen.

Chapter 9

When Hayley pulled onto the Redmond Estate in Northeast Harbor she was taken aback by the colorful spring flowers that were being tended by four gardeners. One wore a fedora type hat to block his eyes from the sun and with a smile tipped it toward Hayley as she drove past him, heading to the main house.

She pulled up in front of the three-story mansion and got out to take in the breathtaking view of the Atlantic and the boats that dotted the harbor, bobbing up and down. She had lived on the island all her life, but still marveled at its unparalleled beauty.

She strolled up the gravel driveway to the front door and rang the bell.

It took almost a minute, but a young woman in a gray dress and white apron opened the door and invited her inside. She led Hayley to a parlor with large open windows that had clear views of the picturesque harbor and offered Hayley something to drink. Hayley politely declined and the young woman disappeared out the door, telling her that Ms. Olivia would be with her momentarily.

Hayley wandered over to the large wall-size bookcase and perused the titles that lined the shelves. Lots of classics and almanacs and books of maps. They were rather dusty and appeared as if they hadn't been touched in decades.

She suddenly heard faint shouting coming from down the hall.

It was a man's voice.

That persistent little voice inside her told her she should stay firmly put. Wait for Olivia to come to her as the young maid had clearly instructed.

But true to form, Hayley's curiosity got the best of her.

She casually walked over to the door and opened it, poking her head out to make sure the coast was clear before quietly following the sound of the bellowing voice, which slowly grew in volume.

About halfway down the hall, she spotted a door that was open a crack.

The man's tirade was at its peak and she could finally make out what he was saying.

"Olivia, you're being absolutely unreasonable."

"I wish you would calm down. Frankly, I'm afraid you're going to hurt yourself with all this yelling."

"Please don't patronize me. I think I deserve better than that."

"I just find your constant nagging tiresome, Thorsten, and you're upsetting Pork Chop, so do try to lower your voice."

"I have worked my fingers to the bone for this company. . . ."

"Playing tennis at the club and dining at expensive

restaurants in New York every night on the company's dime?"

"You know I've given my life to Redmond Meats. Starting out in the mail room, working my way up, proving to your father I would be a worthy successor some day. . . ."

"And I'm sorry I surprised everyone by choosing to take a more active role and unfortunately scuttling your plans."

"It's not that. I think it's great you took over. You have a relaxed style and everybody loves you."

"Not everybody . . ." Olivia said, an ominous tone in her voice.

"But I have been working on these expansion plans for years, with your father's blessing I might add, and I strongly believe *now* is the time. We need to strike while we're on top, and I just need your tie-breaking vote to make it happen."

"And I've told you, I'm not quite ready to make a decision yet. I'm sorry you flew all the way to Maine to hear this—I wish you had just called—but I'm not going to change my mind. At least in the foreseeable future."

"Olivia, I'm begging you. . . ."

"My grandfather built this company from the ground up, and my father was a very successful steward, and now that I am in charge, I'm not going to make any half-cocked decisions until I have carefully considered all the options. And I need more time."

"Half-cocked? Is that what you think this plan is?"

"I'm sorry, Thorsten."

Hayley felt a finger tapping the back of her shoulder.

"Are you lost, ma'am?"

Hayley whipped around, startled.

Mostly startled by someone calling her "ma'am."

It was the fresh-faced young maid who had escorted her to the parlor.

Although now she didn't look so fresh faced.

She looked pretty grim.

"I'm sorry, I was looking for the bathroom. . . ."

The maid cocked her head to one side, utterly unconvinced. "Would you please follow me back to the parlor, ma'am? As I told you, Ms. Olivia will be with you shortly."

There it was again—"ma'am."

Hayley just wanted to slap her.

"What's going on out there?" Olivia said from inside.

Hayley held her breath.

She was about to be fired as the company blogger and she hadn't even started yet.

With a frown the young maid pushed past Hayley and eased open the door. "I'm sorry, Ms. Olivia. I just happened upon this lady hovering outside your office. I told her to wait in the parlor."

There was a brief moment of silence.

Hayley couldn't hold her breath anymore. On an exhale she popped her head inside the room and waved awkwardly at Olivia.

"Oh, Hayley, I'm glad you're here. Come in."

Olivia didn't seem the least bit concerned that Hayley had been eavesdropping.

Hayley smiled at the maid and gingerly stepped

around her into the office where Olivia stood behind a large oak desk. The man who had been yelling, this Thorsten, gazed out the window at the view, lost in his thoughts, grinding his teeth, hardly noticing there were more people in the room. He was tall and slim, with slicked back black hair and a handsome face. He was in a blue blazer, white shirt, and khakis and deck shoes.

Pretty much dressed for sailing.

"That will be all. Thank you."

Grimacing, the maid backed out, not taking her eyes off Hayley.

And Hayley didn't blame her one bit.

"Hayley, I'd like you to meet Thorsten Brandt, our senior vice president of Business Development," Olivia said.

Thorsten turned his attention to Hayley, put on the biggest, brightest smile he could muster, and bounded over and grabbed her hand. "Pleasure to meet you, Hayley. Olivia has been singing your praises. I think it is an excellent idea to have you write recipes for our Web site, give it a personal touch. Welcome to the Redmond family."

This one certainly was a charmer when he wanted to be.

He quickly looked her up and down, his smile dissolving into a wolfish grin, but then it was gone as fast as it came, and he turned back to Olivia.

"I would like to continue this conversation at dinner, if you do not mind, Olivia," he said.

"But I do mind, Thorsten. That's what I've been trying to tell you. This discussion is over," Olivia said, her back arched, her voice dripping with a haughty rage that Hayley had first seen at the Blooming Rose.

When Olivia Redmond had run out of patience, the best thing you could do was run for cover.

Thorsten nodded, too angry to speak, and marched out of the room in a huff, slamming the door behind him.

Olivia watched him go and then turned back to Hayley with a warm smile. "Now, sit down, Hayley. I want to hear all your ideas about what you're going to write about and— Oh, I almost forgot. . . ."

Olivia tore a check off a register and handed it to Hayley. "Here's your advance for the first month."

Hayley glanced at the amount.

Sixteen hundred dollars.

She looked again.

The amount was still sixteen hundred dollars.

"We agreed on two hundred dollars a column twice a week. This is for the first month. I hope that's sufficient," Olivia said.

Hayley guessed that if she said it was not sufficient, Olivia would be writing her an even larger check.

But at the moment, Hayley could barely speak. She was already spending the sixteen hundred dollars in her head.

She couldn't believe her luck.

She stayed well over an hour talking about her favorite bacon recipes. Olivia laughed and clapped her hands and was delighted with all her ideas. It was a great meeting of the minds. Olivia owned a company that sold bacon and Hayley loved any dish with bacon in it.

They were going to make an unbeatable team.

Olivia wrapped things up around six-thirty because she wanted to sit on her porch and have a cocktail before dinner.

Hayley took her cue and left.

The young maid held the front door open for her, glaring at her as she walked out of the house and to her car. As she slid into the driver's seat still under the watchful gaze of the suspicious maid, who was determined to make sure she actually left, Hayley noticed she had left her cell phone on the passenger's seat.

There were nine messages from Liddy.

She called her back as she drove off the Redmond Estate and Liddy picked up on the first ring.

"Where the hell have you been? I've been calling you for the last hour."

"I had a meeting with Olivia Redmond. What is it? What's going on?"

"You are not going to believe this," Liddy gasped.

"What? What?"

"You know my favorite earrings? The ones with the ladybugs that I bought in Paris, not the butterfly ones I picked up in London last summer?"

"Yes, what about them?"

"Well, one of the clasps came loose so I took it into Dawson's Jewelry Store on Main Street to see if they could fix it, and guess who was there."

"I really don't have time to guess, Liddy, it's been a long day. . . ."

She didn't even wait for Hayley to try. "Aaron!"

"My Aaron?"

"Yes! And he was looking at engagement rings! When he saw me come in, he pretended he wasn't, but I saw him standing right in front of the case pointing to one and talking to Mr. Dawson."

"So you think . . . ?"

"We were right, Hayley! He's going to pop the question!"

Chapter 10

Hayley poured the last of the coffee into her mug, the one with a picture of her dog, Leroy, on the side, and shook the round glass pot to make sure she got every last drop.

Boy, did she need caffeine this morning.

She had been up all night writing her first blog for Olivia Redmond.

Writing a paragraph.

Then deleting it.

Writing it again.

Deleting it again.

She wanted her first blog entry to be eye catching and interesting, with an appetizing recipe to get a fevered discussion going online. If she banged out a hurried, run-of-the-mill column and posted it, and it just lay there garnering very few hits, then she would be done working for the Redmond Meats Web site barely after she had begun. This wasn't the *Island Times*.

Sal was very forgiving if on occasion one of her columns was rushed.

Besides, she was also juggling office manager duties in addition to serving as the paper's food-and-cocktails writer.

But Redmond Meats was big business. This was a Fortune 500 company. Screw up once, and she would be out. Despite the CEO's fondness for her recipes.

Hayley had settled on a Bacon Strip Pancakes dish, one she was certain Olivia would drool over. She wrote about how her grandmother used to make them back when Hayley was a teenage girl worried about her weight and yet still couldn't resist them.

It was a sentimental and sweet story, and there was an aching in Hayley's heart as she wrote it because she still missed her father's mother, who had died way back in 1997. She knew Olivia wanted to approve the story before it was posted on the site because she had sent Hayley an e-mail around dinnertime the night before requesting she get it by morning so it could be up on the site by noon eastern time.

So Hayley had e-mailed the blog entry to her at six-thirty in the morning after polishing it one last time. Now it was after eight and she was trying to stay awake to make it through the day.

When she hadn't heard anything by lunchtime, Hayley sent Olivia another e-mail to confirm she had received her original e-mail with the attachment.

She didn't hear anything back.

By three o'clock, she checked the Redmond Meats Web site.

No sign of her tasty Bacon Strip Pancakes recipe. There was a brief bit about Hayley joining the

Redmond Meats family with a small, amazingly flattering photo of her off to the right, but that was it.

Hayley picked up the phone and called the Redmond Estate.

No one picked up.

Not even the maid.

She just got a voice mail message asking to leave her name and number.

By five, it was quitting time. It had been an unusually quiet day. No fires or arrests or car accidents on Route 3.

Sal had spent most of the day in his office on the phone following up on a corruption tip surrounding a state senator.

Bruce had been out all day presumably following leads in the missing Jackson Lab scientist story.

The rest of the staff was out as well, including the sales reps hustling business and the reporters and staff photographers covering local stories and snapping pictures at the girls' softball team's home game.

So no one was around when Hayley cleared out her in-box, shut down her computer, grabbed her purse, and fled out the door to her car.

Remarkably, the engine roared to life on the first turn of the key, which was rare these days, and she drove out of town to the Redmond Estate.

When she pulled up in front of the main house, she spotted the young maid with whom she had tussled earlier. The girl was locking the front door with a key. She turned in time to see Hayley jump out of her car.

"Hi . . . Excuse me, I forgot your name," Hayley

said, trying to be as pleasant as possible since the maid wasn't exactly a fan.

Sure enough, she grimaced and said flatly, "Caroline."

"Yes, Caroline. How could I forget?"

"Because you never asked before and I never told you."

Hayley let that one slide by because the girl was right.

"Could you tell me if Olivia is inside? I know I didn't call first, but I've been trying to reach her all day and it's kind of important."

Caroline shrugged. "I don't know. She was in her office this morning—I heard her on the phone when I was dusting—but then I think she took Pork Chop out for a walk. I didn't hear her come back, so I just assumed they went into town and haven't returned yet."

Hayley scanned the grounds, settling on a detached garage opposite the main house. The garage doors were open, revealing a silver Rolls Royce parked inside. "Isn't that her car right over there?"

Caroline glanced over at the Rolls and she suddenly looked slightly unsettled. "Yes."

"So she probably didn't drive into town."

"She could've gotten a ride with one of the groundskeepers. They usually quit around three and sometimes she'll have one take her to the market so she doesn't have to go to the trouble of taking the Rolls out and finding the right parking spot. She's very particular about where she parks her Rolls because she's afraid of someone parking too close to it and scratching the side."

"I see. That's probably it," Hayley said.

The girl wanted to leave, but was unsure if she should leave Hayley unsupervised given what had happened the last time, when she caught her poking around where she wasn't supposed to.

"Is there anything else?" she asked, eyeing Hayley suspiciously.

"No. But I think I'm going to hang around out here for a while and wait to see if she comes back. Like I said, it's kind of important."

Caroline nodded and then reflexively turned to make sure the door to the main house was locked tight. After firmly jiggling the large brass knob, she brushed past Hayley and walked to a small, beat-up maroon Honda Accord that was parked around the side of the house. It took three tries before the girl got the tired, wheezing motor running. She then shifted the car into reverse and backed out, nearly knocking Hayley down before peeling away—the tires kicking up small pebbles from the gravel driveway, one nearly taking Hayley's eye out—before she drove up to the main road, turned right, and disappeared.

Hayley wondered where Olivia and Pork Chop could have gone. Even if she had taken her pet pig into town with one of the groundskeepers around three o'clock, it was already past five-thirty.

Unless she had never gone to town.

Caroline had told her Olivia had taken Pork Chop for a walk earlier that morning and she had not heard them come back.

So what if she hadn't come back? What if she

was still wandering around in the estate gardens somewhere?

Hayley strolled over to the expansive gardens that made up over half the property, a woodland and flower oasis with azaleas, rhododendrons, and lilacs lining the small dirt path that led to the center, and a white gazebo next to a natural pond all with the crystal blue Atlantic ocean as a backdrop. It was stunning, and with a light breeze, it was quiet and peaceful.

Hayley paused for a moment and stared at the view. She still couldn't believe sometimes she actually lived in the heart of such incredible natural beauty.

She felt something cold and wet on her leg, snapping her out of her reverie.

She didn't jump this time because she was now familiar with this particular feeling and the low grunting that accompanied it.

Hayley looked down to see Pork Chop sniffing her leg. He was covered in dry mud and still wore the diamond-studded collar with the leash attached, which was also caked in dirt.

"Pork Chop, what happened to you?"

She bent down to pet the pig, whose eyes were wide with panic. As she reached out with her hand, the pig backed away. But he wasn't frightened of her.

He was upset.

He waddled in the opposite direction, dragging the leash behind him.

Hayley stood up and followed him deeper into the gardens.

The sun vanished behind a thicket of trees as

Hayley came upon a small patch of grass in a shaded area away from the blooming spring flowers.

Pork Chop ran so far ahead of her she lost sight of him momentarily, but then she heard a wailing sound. It was an agonizing cry, as if the poor pig was in pain. She followed the sound and came upon a muddy area where a sprinkler system was timed to shower the foliage and grass. There she saw Pork Chop circling around a body lying facedown in a mud puddle.

It was a woman.

Her long flower print skirt was hiked up just above her knees, her short-sleeved white blouse was stained and dirty, and her bare arms were akimbo.

Hayley gasped.

There was no question who it was, judging by the inconsolable behavior of Pork Chop, who continued wailing and snorting.

This was bacon heiress Olivia Redmond.

And she was very much dead.

Island Food & Spirits
by
Hayley Powell

My grandmother used to make my brother and me the most delicious Bacon Strip Pancakes when we were kids. I carried on this tradition, whipping them up for my own kids as soon as they could eat solid food.

Because, after all, who wouldn't love a crispy strip of bacon covered with a little pancake batter, then grilled to perfection before being dipped in a bowl of warmed real maple syrup?

Am I right, people?

One time I tried to impress the Ladies Auxiliary by serving them at their 2010 Mount Desert Island Hospital breakfast benefit, but things didn't exactly go according to plan. I cringe at the memory.

I was home relaxing one evening after work with a nerve-calming orange-juice-cranberry vodka cocktail when my phone rang. It was the Ladies Auxiliary president, Mrs. Cunningham, calling to ask if I would be so kind to contribute a dish to their fund-raiser breakfast the following Saturday. Of course I was flattered and immediately accepted, and perhaps fueled by the strong cocktail in my hand, heard myself volunteering to make my grandmother's Bacon Strip Pancakes for everyone who attended if I could have access to the hospital's kitchen. Mrs. Cunningham was thrilled. She offered to provide all the bacon, which was a relief since the price of bacon had recently spiked at the Shop 'n Save.

Ever the organized chef, I prepared my batter the night before and poured it into a large container. With a black marker I wrote my name on the side and also labeled it "pancake batter" and then drove it over to the hospital kitchen where I placed it in the fridge overnight. I would return in the morning at 6:00 AM to get a head start frying the bacon before the breakfast at 8:00 AM.

The perfect plan. *If* I had remembered to set my alarm clock when I went to bed that night. By the time I opened one eye to see the clock, it was already past 7:00 AM! I jumped out of bed and ran around the bedroom, grabbing clothes, slapping on makeup, tying my hair in a ponytail, grabbing my keys, and hightailing it to the car.

I arrived at the hospital in record time, squealing into a free parking space, berating myself for nearly blowing my first chance to participate in one of the town's favorite hospital fund-raisers. Racing into the kitchen out of breath, I did a quick survey. Pounds and pounds of bacon were already sizzling on the giant flattop grill manned by a few of the auxiliary women volunteers. A big sigh of relief! After a quick apology, I hurried to the refrigerator, proud of myself for having the foresight to prepare the pancake batter ahead of time. But then I swung open the refrigerator door and just stared at the empty shelf. The batter wasn't there. I spun around and spotted the marked container sitting on the counter. Another sigh of relief! But when I scurried over to pick it up, I realized the container was empty!

At that moment, Rosie, the weekend breakfast cook, sailed through the door into the kitchen.

"Rosie!" I shrieked, probably a tad too loud as the poor woman nearly jumped out of her skin. I asked about the pancake batter, and with a big grin, Rosie thanked me profusely. She saw my name marked on the side of the container, so she knew who was responsible for dropping off such a delicious treat for the children in the sick ward, at least those who didn't have special dietary needs. The kids loved them and she made sure they all knew I was the one who had so generously donated the batter.

My heart sank. I covered, of course, by plastering a big smile on my face and telling Rosie it was my pleasure. Anything to brighten the day of those sick kids!

Well, I may have been Saint Hayley in the eyes of Rosie and the kids, but that certainly wasn't going to help me with the Ladies Auxiliary. I asked the volunteers to start loading the cooked bacon in the waiting chaffing dishes as I ran to the pantry and scanned the shelves. And then I saw my salvation! A whole shelf completely stocked with those little boxes of prepackaged breakfast cereals! I snatched as many as I could and dumped them into a wheeling cart, and then burst through the swinging doors, pushing the cart, and started hurling the boxes of cereal in the air to the startled people who were trying to catch them. It was as if I was on a Fourth of July parade float in the middle of summer tossing candy to the kids!

But in the end, it all worked out,

and thankfully no one asked for their money back. And the bacon, by the way, was delicious!

Here's the good news! I was asked to help out at the 2011 benefit breakfast, but I was only allowed to serve the juice and coffee. I'm keeping my fingers crossed that eventually I may be able to work my way back up to actually serving a dish one day! Never stop dreaming!

Before sharing my grandmother's Bacon Strip Pancakes recipe, let's enjoy a wonderful cocktail recipe I used to have all the time when I was a young single gal! Yes, the same one who got me into that whole mess!

Madras Cocktail

<u>Ingredients</u>
1½ ounces of your favorite vodka
3 ounces of cranberry juice
1 ounce orange juice

In a cocktail glass filled with ice, add the vodka and cranberry juice. Top off with the orange juice and stir. Then just sit back and remember the good old days!

My Grandmother's Bacon Strip Pancakes

<u>Ingredients</u>
12 slices of your favorite bacon
    cooked crisp on a medium-high
    heat electric griddle.

<u>Easy Homemade Pancake Batter</u>
1 egg
1¼ cup buttermilk (I almost never
    have buttermilk, so just add one
    tablespoon of vinegar to the
    1¼ cup milk, stir, and let stand
    five minutes before using in
    recipe.)
2 tablespoons vegetable oil
1 cup all-purpose flour
1 tablespoon sugar
2 teaspoons baking powder
½ teaspoon baking soda
½ teaspoon salt

In a mixing bowl add the egg and
beat with a fork. Mix in the buttermilk
and vegetable oil. Set aside.

In a large mixing bowl add the
flour, sugar, baking powder, baking
soda, salt and mix together.

Add the egg mixture to the flour
mixture and mix until just blended together.

When you make your batter use a
little less water or milk than you usually

do to make a thicker batter; this will prevent the batter from running all over the place.

After bacon is cooked, remove from griddle and wipe the grease from the griddle. Return half the bacon back to the griddle and place it about two inches apart, then carefully pour batter over each slice of bacon. Once browned, carefully flip the pancake over and brown the other side. Serve with butter and warmed maple syrup.

You're welcome.

Chapter 11

"Olivia Redmond didn't have a heart attack from eating greasy bacon all her life," Sergio said as he walked through Hayley's back door into the kitchen. She and Randy were sitting in her high back chairs next to the counter sipping Mexican Martinis. "She died from a broken neck."

Hayley slammed down her cocktail glass. "Somebody killed her?"

"Snapped it like a tooth," Sergio said, closing the door behind him as he eyed the scrumptious looking cocktails that were now half gone.

"Twig, honey. Snapped her neck like a twig," Randy said, jumping down off the chair and reaching for the bottle of vodka. "Here, let me make you a martini."

"Thank you. It's been a long day."

Poor Sergio had just spent the last six hours securing the crime scene and launching his investigation into Olivia's untimely death.

It was already half past midnight.

After being questioned at the scene, Hayley had

been allowed to drive back to Bar Harbor. She had called her brother on her cell to meet her at the house because she did not want to be alone at this time, and she knew with Sergio busy at the scene and his bar manager, Michelle, handling business at Drinks Like A Fish, Randy would otherwise be at his house all by himself.

Randy rushed right over to find Hayley in a shell-shocked state. Her hands shook as she tried to make them a drink, so Randy gently directed her to a chair and took over. They had been downing Hayley's Mexican Martinis since nine-thirty and had no intention of stopping. Still, though loopy with a slight slur in her voice, she was very alert because she was still haunted by the image in her head of Olivia sprawled out dead in her own garden.

They had been waiting for Sergio to swing by when he was done and pick his husband up to take him home.

"Who would do such a thing?" Hayley wondered as she finished off the last of her martini just as Randy handed Sergio a full one and scooped up Hayley's empty glass to make her another.

"I'm sure there is no shortage of suspects," Randy said, measuring out vodka in a shot glass before giving up and just pouring directly from the bottle. "Olivia Redmond had a lot of money. And people with a lot of money usually have a lot of enemies. That's how they got so rich."

"We're looking into everybody who knew her. Her business associates, her family and friends, the people who worked for her at the estate. It's a long list," Sergio said, yawning.

After one last round so Sergio didn't have to drink

alone, Hayley didn't have to hint that she was tired and wanted to go to bed because she was literally nodding off at the kitchen table, exhausted from the traumatic events of the day.

Randy and Sergio polished off their drinks and each gave her a kiss good night before heading out the door. On his way out, Sergio promised to call and keep her informed with any new developments in the case.

Having a brother-in-law as chief of police certainly had its privileges.

She dragged herself upstairs to her bedroom where she found Leroy curled up and nestled into a pillow by the headboard. As she began to undress, she suddenly heard the doorbell ring downstairs.

She checked the clock on her nightstand.

It was 1:16 AM.

Who would show up on her doorstep at this hour?

She threw on some gray sweatpants and a ratty old T-shirt and padded down the stairs in her bare feet, flipping on a light switch that illuminated the foyer. She paused at the door, unsure if she should open it. Sergio had just told her Olivia Redmond was murdered, so she was understandably jumpy and on edge.

"Who is it?" Hayley called out, loud enough to stir Blueberry, who was stretched out on a recliner in the living room. He gave Hayley a sleepy, annoyed look before closing his eyes again and resting his chin on his paw.

Leroy was still snoozing soundly upstairs.

So much for having a guard dog.

She heard someone talking but couldn't make out the words.

It sounded like a woman's voice.

Finally, she unlatched the lock and opened the door a crack.

Standing on the porch was a wide-eyed, rather rotund woman no more than five feet tall with dull gray frizzy hair. She wore a Japanese print kimono and sandals that barely fit on her pudgy feet. She was heavily made up with too much rouge and smeared lipstick. She looked like one of those scary dolls in a horror movie that moves back and forth in a rocking chair just staring at you.

Hayley hated those movies and the sight of this woman made her shudder.

"I'm so sorry to bother you. But I must speak to you," the woman said, her squeaky, innocent, non-threatening little girl voice putting Hayley at ease.

Just a little bit.

"How can I help you?"

"I've seen you around town but we've never been formally introduced. I'm Madame Flossie."

Madame Flossie. Hayley had heard of her. She was a local eccentric.

A self-professed animal psychic.

And resident crank.

Madame Flossie had set up shop in her tiny apartment above one of the summer tourist shops on Main Street and welcomed pet owners visiting the island from all over who wanted to know why their cat refused to eat dry food or why their dog decided to chew the corner of a brand new area rug.

No one took her psychic readings seriously, but her business was thriving because there was entertainment value in her conclusions. People loved her speculating on what their pet was thinking.

And she made enough money to pay all her bills.

Hayley shook her hand. "Yes. Hello, Flossie. I mean Madame Flossie."

"I would never disturb you at such a late hour, but I've been listening to all the reports on my police scanner at home about the awful events that happened at the Redmond Estate."

"Yes. It's very tragic," Hayley said, still clueless why this woman was standing on her doorstep at one in the morning.

"Is he here?"

"Who?"

"The potbellied pig."

"You mean Pork Chop?"

"Yes."

"No. I'm afraid the police took him over to Dr. Palmer's vet clinic for an examination earlier this evening and he's being kept there until they can figure out what to do with him."

"I see. It's vitally important I speak with him."

"Doctor Palmer?"

"No. The pig."

"You want to . . . talk to Pork Chop?"

"Yes. He may have witnessed Olivia Redmond's murder. He may be able to give me a description of her killer."

Hayley just stood there, dumbfounded.

She was skeptical to be sure. But she was also intrigued.

"So can you help me get access to the pig so I can

question him?" Madame Flossie asked, wringing her hands, her eyes as big as saucers.

It was the silliest idea Hayley had ever heard.

And yet she found herself saying yes.

She was going to help Madame Flossie have a psychic sit down with a murder witness who just happened to be a potbellied pig.

Chapter 12

Aaron couldn't stop laughing on the other end of the phone.

Hayley sighed. "Fine. Get it out. I'll wait."

She had called him the moment she got to the office the following morning, and after explaining how Madame Flossie wanted to come by his clinic to have a psychic chat with Pork Chop, the potbellied pig, the giggles erupted and had yet to subside.

"Look, I know it sounds ridiculous, but the woman was pretty adamant, and who knows, she may find out something valuable."

"From the pig?" Aaron asked, his voice cracking as he let loose with another machine gun spurt of laughter.

"Look, she may very well be a kook, but what do we have to lose?"

"Oh, I don't know, my reputation, perhaps? Especially if word gets out I'm having séances at my practice and talking to the animals like Dr. Dolittle!"

"Nobody has to know."

She could see Aaron shaking his head in disbelief

on the other end of the phone, probably raking a hand through his wavy brown hair as he considered the risk he was taking if someone were to be tipped off about Pork Chop's psychic interrogation at his vet clinic.

She had been waiting for the right moment to call him, perhaps reconnect again after he brushed her off when she showed up at his office earlier in the week. So why on earth had she chosen this hare-brained scheme to get him on the phone so she could hear his voice?

"If it's too much, maybe I can just check him out of the clinic and take him over to my house after work and do it there?" Hayley said, now embarrassed she had even called him.

"No, he's been very stressed and skittish since the cops brought him in here, and his blood pressure is off the charts. I want to keep him here so I can monitor his vitals. He's clearly traumatized by what happened to Ms. Redmond."

"So your answer is no?"

There was a long pause as he considered.

Aaron chuckled. "I guess there's no harm in letting this Madame Flora . . ."

"Flossie. Madame Flossie."

"Whatever. Tell her she can come by around lunchtime. I'll let her use my spare exam room, and she has no more than twenty minutes with him."

"Thank you, Aaron."

"And I want you here to make sure she doesn't do anything too nutty. Up until today, this has been a respectable business. I'm going to be busy with other patients and won't be able to keep an eye on her."

"I'll be there," Hayley said.

"If Pork Chop in any way gets upset or anxious, I want you to shut it down."

"Got it."

"Oh, and Hayley?"

"Yes."

"You owe me."

He hung up before explaining what exactly that meant. She would happily repay this favor with a home-cooked meal or a night out at the movies. She missed their dates.

She still couldn't fathom Liddy's notion that Aaron was getting ready to propose.

It was too preposterous.

They hadn't been seeing each other all that long.

No. Impossible.

But Hayley also knew that most times when she made her mind up so firmly about something not happening there was a strong likelihood that it actually would happen.

She was a terrible psychic. Hopefully Madame Flossie would be a better one.

If only she could read people and not just animals. Maybe Hayley would be clued in to what was in store for her immediate future.

But the question of who killed Olivia Redmond was a far more important question than whether or not Dr. Aaron was about to ask her to marry him.

She picked up the phone and called Madame Flossie at the number she had given her the night before to set up the appointment.

When Hayley pulled up in front of Aaron's office across town a couple hours later, Madame Flossie was already outside the door waiting for her, pacing back and forth, a lost look in her eye, like her mind was somewhere else.

Hayley got out of her car and slowly approached her. "Madame Flossie?"

Her head jerked and her eyes rolled. She was wearing a green and white scarf on her head and a matching muumuu that draped over her full-figured form. Her pudgy hands were clasped together.

Hayley placed a hand gently on her shoulder. "Is everything all right?"

Madame Flossie suddenly snapped out of her trance and looked at Hayley with big round doe eyes. "Yes. Everything is fine. There is just a lot of energy going on right now. I'm picking up the thoughts of many animals inside who are dying to talk to someone. Mostly to complain about their owners."

"Shall we go inside?"

Madame Flossie nodded and followed as Hayley pushed open the door, and they entered the waiting room of the clinic. There was just one elderly woman sitting in a chair with her rag doll cat in her lap, stroking his back.

Aaron's Nazi receptionist, Edna, nodded courteously with a tight smile and waved them through the door leading back to the exam rooms. She didn't look too happy about having to cooperate and cater to this obvious pair of whack jobs. "Dr. Palmer sends his apologies. He's very busy today so he won't be able to stop by and say hello."

That was her way of saying, *Dr. Palmer has no intention of actually taking time out of his day to indulge in this freak show.*

"It's just as well," Madame Flossie said, almost dismissively. "We need privacy. Pork Chop will be more likely to open up to me if there isn't a crowd around."

"Should I wait outside?" Hayley asked, hoping she would say yes.

"No. You're fine, Hayley. Pork Chop already knows you. You might be a source of comfort."

"I'll go get the pig," Edna said before closing the door.

Madame Flossie floated about the room, looking around and taking in deep breaths.

Hayley hovered in the corner, trying desperately not to get in the way.

A few minutes later Edna returned with Pork Chop.

Aaron was right. Pork Chop appeared nervous and unsettled as Edna set him down on the cold steel exam table.

"Let me know if you need anything else," Edna said, an exasperated edge to her voice as she gave the two women one last long withering stare and left the room.

"Pork Chop doesn't like her," Madame Flossie said as she delicately scratched the pig underneath his chin.

"I'm sorry?"

"The receptionist. Pork Chop thinks she's a bitch."

Hayley laughed. "Are you sure you're not channeling *me* right now?"

Madame Flossie ignored her. She was focused on Pork Chop, who was moving around, restless and shaky.

"Yes. I understand."

"Understand what?"

"Shhhh. Please, Hayley. Don't interrupt. Pork Chop is talking."

"Oh. Sorry."

She half expected the pig's mouth to be moving.

Hayley had always imagined that if an animal spoke, it would be like in the countless Disney animated movies she had bought for her kids on DVD.

"He misses her so much. He loved Ms. Redmond. Except for the times she would leave him in the care of her servants to take trips with her husband. He would suffer separation anxiety and lose his appetite until she returned. But the servants never told her how upset he was when she was gone; they would always just say he was fine and no trouble. He didn't like them lying like that."

Hayley stepped a little closer. She was intrigued.

"Oh my. Now, there's no need to be so vulgar."

"What did he say?"

"He clearly does not like Olivia's husband, Nacho. He just called him a money-grubbing man whore."

"Wow. Pork Chop actually said 'man whore'?"

Madame Flossie nodded. "Yes. He says Ms. Redmond used to leave the TV on to keep him company when she went out, so he learned a lot from *The Real Housewives*."

Hayley stifled a giggle.

Maybe Aaron was right and this was just a bunch of time-wasting malarky.

Madame Flossie held the pig's chin. He was staring straight into her eyes, transfixed, or as the pet psychic would have her believe, having a very intense conversation.

"Is that so? He's saying he saw what happened to

Ms. Redmond. Someone came up behind her and grabbed her in a choke hold and twisted her neck until it snapped."

Pretty close to how Sergio had described what happened.

"It was a man. A man killed Olivia according to Pork Chop," Madame Flossie said, leaning down so the pig could sniff the tip of her nose. "There, there, it's okay to cry. You've suffered a tremendous loss."

Hayley, despite her skepticism, was transfixed. She had already been told once to keep quiet, but she just couldn't resist another outburst. "Was it Olivia's husband? Was it Nacho?"

Madame Flossie picked up the potbellied pig in her arms and pressed him into her chest. "There. There. Let it out. Let it all out."

She then turned to Hayley. "No. The husband had nothing to do with the crime. But Pork Chop was very clear about one thing. The killer was a stranger. He had never laid eyes on him before."

Chapter 13

"So you were a friend of my mother's?" the young man said, barely above the drinking age of twenty-one. His shoulder-length brown hair was pulled back in a ponytail and a maroon tank top hung over his bony frame. He was wearing baggy jeans that hung low on his waist and there was a Doctor Who phone booth tattoo on his left shoulder that gave the impression he was at least slightly more interesting than he appeared.

Hayley held out her hand. "Yes. I'm Hayley Powell. You must be Edward."

He leaned against the door, casually eating some potato salad from a plastic container before finally taking her hand and shaking it. Then he quickly withdrew it and wiped the palm of his hand on the front of his tank top.

Hayley cleared her throat, breaking the uncomfortable silence. "Your mother and I had only met recently. She hired me to write a blog for the Redmond Meats Web site."

"Oh. So you're here to get paid? How much did she owe you?"

"No," Hayley said, mortified. "I'm not here for money. I heard you had arrived in town and so I just wanted to stop by and offer my condolences."

"I see," the boy said suspiciously.

"Who is it?" a girl's scratchy voice cooed from behind the door.

"Someone who worked for my mother."

A shapely woman, no more than eighteen years old, popped into the doorway and slid underneath the boy's arm. She was a foot shorter than he was but round and curvaceous, the exact opposite of his wiry frame. She wore a light green sundress and a flower in her curly blond hair like some sixties flower child dancing through Haight-Ashbury. She twisted a long strand of her golden locks around her finger and pushed her pouty lips out as she gave Hayley the once-over.

"I'm Peggy," she said.

"Hayley. Nice to meet you."

"This is my girlfriend," Edward said needlessly, as the girl was clinging to him like a lost puppy who had just been found by her owner in the woods.

There was a moment of awkward silence.

"Would you like to come in for some tea?" Peggy blurted out, surprising her boyfriend, who gave a look that seemed to say, *For the love of God, please shut up!*

"No, thank you," Hayley said. "I know this must be a difficult time for both of you and I don't want to intrude. . . ."

"We've only been here a few hours and I'm already going stir crazy in this big old empty house!

Please! We have real Earl Grey British tea! Not that watered down American Lipton crap," Peggy said excitedly.

Hayley glanced at Edward, who had given up. It was apparently easier for him to just bend to his girl-friend's will, so he simply forced a smile. "Yes. Come in."

"Well, maybe for a few minutes . . ."

Peggy clapped her hands and pushed the door all the way open, allowing Hayley to step inside before turning to Edward.

"What's the maid's name again?"

"Cathy, I think," Edward said, shrugging.

"Caroline. I believe it's Caroline," Hayley corrected him.

"Okay. Let's try that! Caroline!" Peggy shrieked so loudly some birds in a tree opposite the main entrance to the estate flapped their wings in a panic and flew high into the sky just as she slammed the door shut.

Caroline walked down the hall toward the foyer, her heels clicking on the hardwood floors. Her eyes narrowed at the sight of Hayley. It was clear she considered her a nosy nuisance and was none too pleased she was now hobnobbing with Olivia's son and girlfriend of the moment.

"We'd like some tea, please, in the parlor," Peggy said, adopting an English accent. "Proper English tea. You'll find it in the pantry."

"Yes, I know where it is," Caroline said flatly before turning on her heel and skulking back to the kitchen.

"Again, Edward, let me just say how sorry I am about your mother," Hayley said as Peggy took her by the arm and led her into the same room where she was escorted the first time she arrived to meet with Olivia.

"It's Red. Everyone calls me Red," he snarled, as if he was annoyed she hadn't guessed his nickname before.

"I'm sorry. Red."

"And let's be clear. Red does not stand for red meat, right, honey? My baby is a strict vegan. Just like me," Peggy said, plopping down on an antique love seat.

"The height of irony," Red scoffed. "Heir to a bacon fortune and I won't even touch the stuff."

"Do you watch *Downton Abbey*?" Peggy asked, leaning forward, her eyes as big as saucers as she stared at Hayley.

Hayley was struck by the sudden change in topic and needed a moment to collect her thoughts. "Yes, I've seen it."

"I love that show! Doesn't this place sort of remind you of the big house they live in? I mean, not the design or anything, but the grandness and the echoey rooms."

"I suppose. . . ." Hayley said, her voice trailing off as she saw not the slightest similarity between this seacoast Maine mansion and Highclere castle in the English countryside.

The next few minutes were a detailed rundown of why Peggy loved *Downton Abbey*. How she never missed an episode. How she modeled her life after the fashionable and proper Lady Mary, which Hayley found amusing because in her opinion, the haughty character of Lady Mary was self-absorbed and spoiled.

Who would *want* to be like that?

Peggy continued prattling on about how now that Red was going to be inheriting his mother's estate, she would be living a parallel life to her fictional heroine, and how marvelous it all was.

Red sat back in a chair next to the love seat his girlfriend was occupying and watched her with a tight smile, indulging her for the moment but ready to intervene if she said too much.

"This place reminds me so much of how Lord and Lady Grantham lived during that time. Except their servants were a lot *nicer*," Peggy spit out as Caroline entered with a tea tray and set it down on a small antique coffee table between them.

Hayley noticed the corners of Caroline's eyes were wet with tears. Either she had been in the kitchen crying over her late employer or, more likely, over the fact that she was now beholden to this crass, gold-digging harpy.

"Thank you, Caroline. That will be all," Peggy said in her most lofty, obnoxious tone.

Caroline cringed and got out of there as fast as she could without being too obvious.

After just a few sips, Red was clearly bored. This was Peggy's little tea party and he wanted no part of it. He set his cup down and stood up. "I have some things to do."

Details to handle regarding my mother's passing . . ."

"Of course, I understand. I should go. . . ."

"No. Please, stay. Keep me company," Peggy begged.

"Finish your tea. It would mean a lot to Peggy," Red said as he walked out.

Peggy put on a frown for full effect. "He's really bummed out by his mother dying."

Bummed out?

Lady Mary would never say anything like that.

And on the surface, at least in Hayley's eyes, Red did not seem the least bit upset by his mother's grisly murder in the garden.

"Were they close?"

Peggy let out a spurt of giggles. She put a hand over her mouth when she noticed Hayley staring at her.

"I'm sorry. That was rude. Just the idea of Red being close to his mother is hysterical. He couldn't stand her!"

"But you just said he was . . . bummed out."

"Yes. Because he's the executioner."

"What?"

"Yes. The executioner of the estate."

"You mean executor," Hayley said, gently correcting her.

Unlike Sergio's malapropisms, which were born out of English being his second language, this flighty nitwit had no legitimate excuse.

"Yeah, I guess. He's her only child and his dad was paid off and kicked to the curb when he divorced Red's mother, so now all the annoying details and boring paperwork is on his shoulders."

"I see."

"My poor baby. Stuck here for God knows how long handling this whole mess. Just when we were scheduled to go to the Coachella music festival in Palm Springs. But between you and me, if I had a choice of standing in the desert baking in the sun, dehydrated, listening to one obscure band after another for three days or hanging out here in the lap of luxury, I'm happy we had to come here!"

Such a sweet, sensitive girl.

"He doesn't even care about getting all that money. Luckily he's got me to look out for him and to make sure he gets what's coming to him. More tea?" Peggy said, lifting the pot from the tray.

"No, thank you, I'm fine."

Peggy didn't wait for Hayley to finish. She poured anyway, filling her cup to the brim.

"Oh. Okay . . ." Hayley said, resigned to the fact she would be stuck here for a little while longer.

"After we first got together Red wanted to take me to Bali for a month, but he didn't have enough money and got angry because he's got a *huge* trust fund, but he can't touch it until he's twenty-five and his mother wouldn't let him withdraw a cent early. I told him what mother who loved her son would deny him his due? Especially when he's met the love of his life and wants to impress her and give her the lifestyle she so richly deserves!"

"You . . . actually said that to him?"

"Yes. Why?" she asked, doe eyed, oblivious to how wretched she was acting.

"No reason. Well, I guess now that Olivia is gone, that's all moot."

"Moot? What's moot?"

"I just meant now he's going to inherit everything, so the trust fund issue is no longer important."

"I know! Isn't it wonderful?" Peggy said, a gleeful look in her eye.

Remarkably, after a moment Peggy must have realized she shouldn't be so giddy over her financial prospects so soon after a woman's death, so she struggled to appear slightly more solemn. "Of course, despite Red's relationship with his mother, it's still all very tragic."

She knew she needed to act more appropriately. Like how Lady Mary mourned when her younger sister, Sybil, died, on *Downton Abbey* in the second season.

That lasted about a minute.

"I saw a Rolls Royce parked in the garage earlier! Would you like to go for a spin?"

"Oh, I can't."

"I asked Caroline where the keys were kept and she pretended not to know, but I could tell she was lying. She just doesn't want me driving it. So I did a little snooping and I found them in a drawer in Olivia's bedroom," Peggy said, fishing them out of a pocket in her sundress and dangling them in front of Hayley. "Come on. It'll be fun."

How Hayley became this obnoxious, odious girl's new best friend was completely beyond her. "Afraid not. I need to go home. I have a column to write for the paper."

Peggy sighed. "Suit yourself."

The girl had zero interest in what kind of column Hayley needed to write or anything else. She was too focused on her joy ride in a Rolls.

Peggy floated out the door, not even offering to show her out.

Hayley stepped into the hallway and was greeted by Red again, who seemed to be having second thoughts about leaving her in the hands of his chatty, gossipy girlfriend.

"I appreciate you stopping by, Hayley," Red said.

No, he didn't. He just wanted to make sure she was going to leave.

"There is one thing I want to discuss with you before I go," Hayley said.

His shoulders tensed. He'd been *so* close to getting rid of her.

"It's about Pork Chop. The vet, Dr. Palmer, is going to release him tomorrow. I know you're probably swamped with funeral arrangements and meetings with lawyers, so I just wanted to say I would be happy to drive him over here myself and drop him off."

"That's very sweet of you, Hayley, but it's not necessary," Red said.

"It's really no problem. . . ."

"The thing is, I don't want him."

"But—"

"My mother showered more gifts and attention on that porker in one week than she ever did on me my entire life. So I have no intention of ever laying eyes on that damn dirty pig ever again!"

Chapter 14

"I'm sorry, Hayley, but I can't keep him here any longer. If someone doesn't claim him soon, I'm going to have to resort to more drastic measures," Aaron said, sitting behind the large oak desk in his office, sleeves rolled up and tie askew.

It had been a long day and he was tired.

"You mean *put him down*?" Hayley gasped.

"No. I mean calling animal control. What they do with him after that, however, I have no say over. I'm sorry."

Aaron's very businesslike behavior was nagging at Hayley, but she chose not to call him on it.

"Well, what should I do?"

"You can always take Pork Chop home with you until you figure out what to do with him," Aaron suggested, rifling through some paperwork and scratching some notes on a pad with a pencil.

He knew from dating Hayley that she was a sentimental sucker and an enthusiastic animal lover, so in his mind the problem had already been solved.

"You know I can't do that. I have two very high

maintenance pets already who take up all of my energy."

"Then I don't know what else to tell you," he said, barely glancing up from the papers on his desk.

"Aaron . . ."

"Yeah?"

He scribbled more notes, his eyes glued to his pad of paper.

Hayley just stood there in silence, debating with herself on what she should say. She really couldn't handle the obvious wall between them much longer.

Propose or break it off.

Just pick one and do it.

For both their sakes.

Aaron finally realized she wasn't talking and looked up. "Did you want to say something, Hayley?"

She cleared her throat. It was time. They needed to discuss their relationship. She was finally in the same room with him. She had his attention. He was curious what she had to say.

Go for it.

Just go for it.

"Do you have a pet carrier I can borrow?"

Aaron gave her a slight smile and nodded.

She could have kicked herself. What a wimp she was.

Fifteen minutes later she was pulling into her driveway. Next to her on the passenger seat Pork Chop was pressing his snout against the wire-rimmed cage, curious as to where he was going. She and Aaron had had no trouble getting him inside the carrier. He was probably grateful to be leaving the clinic where he was housed with a bunch of loud barking dogs.

Hayley got out of the car and circled around to lift the carrier out and haul her new houseguest inside.

Leroy bounded down the steps, his toenails that needed to be clipped clicking on the hardwood floors as he scurried into the kitchen to greet Hayley. His tail wagged excitedly as Hayley bent down to rub the fur on top of his head, and his tongue hung out of his mouth as he panted. He gazed at Hayley, trying his best to look adorable and devoted so she might feed him before pouring herself a glass of wine.

That's when the snorting from the animal carrier she had set down on the floor diverted his attention. Hayley unlatched the lock on the cage and opened the door, and Pork Chop tentatively poked his head out to take in his new surroundings.

"We're going to have company for a few days, Leroy. This is Pork Chop. Try to make him feel at home."

Leroy was startled by this noisy creature with black skin, erect ears, and a short snout. At first he recoiled, finding cover behind Hayley's leg, but his curiosity got the best of him and he couldn't help but slowly approach the pig, who was already inhaling bits of food that had fallen underneath the kitchen table.

Hayley tried looking on the bright side. Maybe she wouldn't have to vacuum as much with a potbellied pig around.

When Leroy got close enough, the pig, who had poor eyesight but excellent hearing and sense of smell, sensed the dog approaching and turned to greet him. Leroy was close enough that his nose touched Pork Chop's snout.

No barking.

No biting.

No panicking.

Just a calm friendly introduction.

Leroy's tail slowly resumed wagging. He had a new playmate.

This temporary arrangement just might work out after all.

And then she heard the hissing.

Her Persian cat, Blueberry, bared his teeth, whiskers curled up doing his best to demonstrate his disapproval. He stood in the doorway to the kitchen, back arched high in the air, or as much as a twenty-pound Persian cat could raise it, eyes locked on the interloper, who at the moment was paying him no mind.

"You're just going to have to get used to him, Blueberry. He's not going anywhere for a few days," Hayley said.

The next two hours were sheer hell.

Hayley had taken a few minutes to pour herself a glass of wine while Pork Chop trotted off to explore the house. He was soon tearing up a quilt on the couch as he tried to find a nesting place. Leroy joined in, believing it was some kind of game. And Blueberry continued hissing and emitting a low steady growl as he kept his distance from the pig. Unfortunately that plan failed when Pork Chop got too close for comfort, so Blueberry lashed out with his claws, slashing the pig's snout, who wailed in pain. Leroy, frightened by the pig's cries, started barking.

Hayley knelt down to comfort the pig and saw a crippling sad look in his eyes as he continued whining. It was clear he wasn't crying from Blueberry's unprovoked attack.

This pig was in mourning.

He was missing his mistress, Olivia Redmond. And her absence was amplified by the fact that he had been deposited from one strange place to another in the span of just a few days.

More wailing.

More hissing.

More barking.

At least her empty-nest syndrome was finally cured. Yes, she still missed the kids. But now her hands were full with a grief-stricken pig, a high-strung dog, and an enraged territorial cat.

Hayley poured herself another glass of wine.

Thankfully, two hours later Randy arrived with a box full of table scraps he had packed up at his bar.

"I know there are all these rules about what pigs should and should not eat, but I figured tonight we could make an exception. At least until you can get to the store and stock up on some healthier vegetation."

"Thank you, Randy. I appreciate it."

She removed the tin foil and made a plate of chicken fingers, French fries, some leftover hamburger meat, and the remnants of a tossed salad and set it down for Pork Chop, who excitedly consumed it, and was soon joined by Leroy, who insisted on his own fair share. Blueberry remained underneath the coffee table in the living room, defiantly making his point that he was not happy about any of this situation by keeping up his low, incessant growl.

"You have a plan yet on what you're going to do with him?"

Hayley shook her head and gulped down her wine. "Olivia's son, Red, wants nothing to do with him."

"Sergio stopped by the bar on his way home. He

had just finished questioning Olivia Redmond's maid. . . ."

"Caroline."

"Right. Anyway, according to her, on the day Olivia was killed, before she took Pork Chop out for a walk and never came back, she had a visitor."

"Who?"

"Felicity Flynn-Chan."

"The owner of the Blooming Rose restaurant?"

"Yes. They talked for about fifteen minutes. Caroline was in the kitchen washing the breakfast dishes and couldn't hear what was said, but she saw Felicity leave and she did not look happy. In fact, it looked like she was crying."

Chapter 15

"Hayley, could you please step into the kitchen where we can speak privately?" Felicity Flynn-Chan squeaked, her face a ghostly white and her hands trembling. "Dora, please show the Rockefeller party to the table near the bay window."

"Yes, Felicity," the wispy hostess said in a whisper. She had on the same sundress she had worn the last time Hayley was at the Blooming Rose and, snatching up a handful of menus, she escorted the three elderly patrons across the dining room.

Felicity gripped Hayley tightly by the shoulder and guided her through the wooden swinging doors into the hot, steamy kitchen where her husband, Alan, was hard at work preparing each dish that was ordered with a small staff of sous-chefs assisting with the chopping and dicing.

"Hayley, do you know who those people were out there?" Felicity said, the veins in her forehead popping out like she was in one of those alien movies where the visitors take human form, revealing themselves at the end of the movie to be lizard people.

"You called them the Rockefellers, so I assume they're related to the ones in Seal Harbor?"

"And you would be correct. They visit the family estate every summer and always make a point of dining here and recommending us to all of their wealthy friends who come to the island."

Hayley nodded, smiling, not sure why it was so important for her to know all this, so she answered with a simple, "I see."

"So you can imagine how awkward it was when you barged in here just as they were about to sit down to have dinner and said in the loudest voice imaginable, 'Felicity, I would like to ask you a few questions about Olivia Redmond's murder!'"

"Oh, I don't think I was that loud. I pride myself on being subtle."

"Subtle? You might as well have been shouting over a stadium of screaming girls at a One Direction concert."

One of the sous-chefs dicing some carrots on a cutting board snickered.

"Felicity, I'm so sorry, but I don't understand. . . ."

"Olivia Redmond's murder is the only thing anyone is talking about. Tongues are wagging and everyone is guessing what happened to her, and you, with a very well-known reputation for insinuating yourself into local investigations, marched into my place of business and announced that I am a suspect. I can't have that! If rumors spread that I have any connection to that sordid business, my business will go belly up! This is our busiest season! Martha Stewart just called today to request a table for twelve for tomorrow night. I don't have a table for twelve. I had to convince her it was a good idea to dine with her friends on the patio alfresco with the black flies! This is my livelihood, Hayley! I depend on my customers! I can't afford a whispering campaign about me being some sort of ruthless killer!"

"I guess when you put it that way I can see why I might have practiced a bit more discretion. . . ."

"Especially since I already spoke with Chief Alvares earlier today, *not* during business hours, mind you, and was able to put the whole matter to rest."

"Oh. I didn't know that."

"Well, maybe you should have better lines of communication so this doesn't happen again."

Hayley felt horrible.

In hindsight, she did just sort of breeze through the front door of Felicity's restaurant and ask her point blank about a murder, not even noticing who was standing around the hostess station or milling about the coatrack.

"Felicity, I really am sorry. . . ."

Hayley knew Felicity was in no mood to share whatever she told Sergio, so she turned to leave quietly before she made the situation any worse. She quietly retreated through the wooden swinging doors back into the main dining room and headed for the door. Felicity followed close behind to ensure she was actually leaving. She probably feared Hayley would go from table to table asking everyone at the restaurant questions about the Olivia Redmond murder.

Almost as an afterthought, Hayley turned and said, "By the way, the leftovers from the other night were scrumptious."

Felicity's demeanor changed instantly. She smiled

warmly. "Why, thank you. That's so sweet of you to say."

Felicity looked around, smiling at a handsome couple waiting to be seated, making sure they heard Hayley's stellar review. "Someone will be with you in a moment."

The couple nodded and within seconds the hostess had menus in her arms and was leading them to a table.

Felicity took Hayley by the arm, this time much more gently, and steered her out the door to the parking lot. "That was a lovely thing to say, Hayley."

"It's the truth."

Felicity stared at Hayley, gauging her sincerity, and once she was convinced, became far more convivial and engaging. "I hope you go online and write a review for us on all those travel Web sites. We rely on our customers' testimonials to get the tourists to try us out."

"I'll be sure to do that," Hayley said.

"I'm sorry I was so cross with you in there. We're very worried about this summer. The projections don't look good so far and all the local businesses are on edge that the summer tourist season is going to be down from last year. None of us can afford any negative publicity."

"I totally get it. I work at the paper. I've read all the reports. I should have been more sensitive to that when I came here."

"That's the reason I went to see Olivia Redmond on the day she was killed," Felicity said. "I didn't want her bad-mouthing the restaurant to all her high society friends, so I paid her a visit to apologize once again and offer to cater one of her summer parties free of charge in an effort to make it up to her."

If Hayley had known complimenting her high end restaurant was a surefire way to get Felicity Flynn-Chan to open up and talk, she would have planned her trip to Town Hill to pump her for information more strategically.

"Of course she turned me down flat," Felicity said, sighing. "She wasn't in a forgiving mood. So I left. I drove back here and spent the rest of the day with my gardener in our vegetable garden just over there, picking out fresh produce for the restaurant's menu that day. Chief Alvares spoke with Barney, who is a respectable local, as you know, and he corroborated my alibi, so I have officially been crossed off the suspect list."

"Again, Felicity, I am so sorry."

"Just promise me you'll come back for dinner here again and bring all your friends."

"Just try to keep me away."

With Felicity's feathers no longer ruffled, Hayley was free to jump in her car and drive back to town. She thought about stopping by the office to finish her column there before heading home, but she knew Bruce was there working late, and frankly she just didn't want to see him. He had been in a terrible state all day when the one lead in his investigation of Dr. Foley's disappearance led him to a dead end.

He was getting nowhere.

And with Olivia Redmond's murder demanding his attention now that the hullabaloo over Hayley's TV appearance had finally subsided, the public's demand for answers in the Foley investigation was rapidly waning.

Bruce felt in his gut that Dr. Foley's disappearance was the result of foul play and the whole matter was now in danger of being completely forgotten.

He was back to square one and enormously frustrated.

Hayley was frustrated as well.

Only one day on her new gig moonlighting as a bona fide bacon blogger and her quick-tempered yet exceedingly generous employer was now dead.

And whoever did the dirty deed had shown no mercy.

She was determined not to let him get away with it.

Island Food & Spirits
by
Hayley Powell

I've had a serious craving for Mexican food all week. Probably because I watched *El Mariachi* on Netflix last weekend. So last night after work I stopped by the Shop 'n Save to pick up the ingredients for my favorite Bacon Nachos. On the drive home, my BFF Liddy called my cell no doubt to tell me how she was getting along with the new friend she had recently made.

For about six months, Liddy had been contemplating adopting a dog that she could love and tote around in one of those cute but expensive dog carriers and dress in some outrageously priced tiny, adorable dog outfits she had found online. My other BFF, Mona, was totally against this pet adoption idea because she hated the thought of some poor animal dressed up and blinged out and totally humiliated. Not to mention the fact Liddy could barely take care of herself let alone one of God's precious creatures. What if she got bored with it and forgot to feed it, or worse, left it behind on one of her shopping sprees at the Bangor Mall?

Mona suggested Liddy volunteer at the local ASPCA in Trenton for a few months just to see if she was suited to the responsibility of being a dog owner. Much to Mona's surprise, and mine, too, Liddy took to the idea and after only an hour on the job, she announced she was bringing home a dog that was recently abandoned at the shelter to foster it for a few weeks before it was put up for adoption in a forever home.

When I asked Liddy on the phone how she was handling being a pet foster mother, she screamed into the phone, "I'll tell you how it's going! I cooked for the dog and now I've killed it! Please! You need to get over here now! I need help!"

Liddy was a terrible cook.

What on earth was she thinking?

I raced over to her house, but kept Liddy on the line to keep her calm. I asked if she had called Aaron, the town vet.

"No! I absolutely do not want the whole world to know I killed a dog with my cooking!" she wailed.

When I arrived at Liddy's house, the front door was unlocked, and as I entered, it was eerily quiet.

"Liddy?"

"In the guest bedroom! Hurry!"

I followed her voice and found her on the bed with Poppy, a rather large black Labrador retriever mix (which she named after her favorite bagel, the Poppy Seed). Liddy was cradling Poppy's head in her lap, and my heart skipped a beat as I looked at the poor dog lying there so still.

As I slowly approached the bed, I could see poor Poppy's stomach rise and fall, so at least I knew she was breathing. Liddy looked so sad and distraught that for once I didn't know what to say.

Suddenly, out of the blue we both began shrieking in horror as Poppy's stomach began poking out in different directions as if it had a life of its own.

Poppy let out a loud, agonizing moan.

"Dear God, Liddy! What in the world did you feed her?"

"Scrambled eggs! I just fed her scrambled eggs!"

It was like that scene in the movie *Alien,* when that gory little slimy creature popped out of that man's stomach!

Poppy kept moaning and panting, stomach rising and falling.

Liddy was now in tears and completely inconsolable. "What have I done? What have I done?"

At that moment, Poppy tensed and, right before our panicked eyes, gave birth to a tiny poppy seed of her own.

"You didn't kill her, Liddy! She's having puppies!"

"Right on my brand new Martha Stewart Somerset Peony comforter!"

"At least she has good taste," I said, smiling.

We settled in for a long night as another puppy began its journey out into the world. I went to my car and grabbed my bag of groceries and fixed us a heaping platter of my Bacon Nachos to help pass the time. I also whipped up a nice cold pitcher of Melon Martinis to wash them down with and calm our nerves.

When all was said and done at two the next morning, Liddy was the proud foster mother of one momma foster dog and twelve darling little foster puppies. I assumed Liddy would hold off on her decision to get her own dog after this harrowing experience, but who knows? She now has thirteen dogs to choose from!

This week I'm sharing my heavenly Bacon Nachos recipe, which is sure to be a hit with all your friends and family. Olé!

Hayley's Bacon Nachos

Ingredients
½ pound of cooked bacon, crumbled
  and divided
½ of a large red onion, chopped and
  divided
One tomato, seeded and chopped
½ cup sliced black olives
5 or 6 jalapeños, seeded and chopped
2 to 3 cups of Mexican blend cheese,
  halved
1 bag of your favorite tortilla chips

Preheat your oven to 400 degrees.
Then line a baking sheet with aluminum foil. Spread half the tortilla
chips on the foil. Sprinkle with half of
the bacon, onion, peppers, and cheese.
Spread on the remaining chips, then
top with the remaining ingredients and
end with the cheese. Bake in the oven
for 10 to 15 minutes, or until cheese is
completely melted and beginning to
slightly brown. Serve with sour cream
and salsa if desired.

Melon Martini

Ingredients
2 ounces your favorite nonflavored
  vodka
½ ounce melon liqueur

½ ounce simple syrup
1 slice melon to garnish

Fill a shaker with ice cubes and then add all your ingredients. Shake and strain into a chilled martini glass. Garnish with the melon slice and be ready to be wowed.

Chapter 16

"Hayley, I want to explain why I've been slightly distant lately," Aaron said.

Slightly?

That was a bit of an understatement.

Hayley took a deep breath. She wiped her mouth with a yellow cloth napkin and set it back down in her lap.

Aaron was nervous and fidgety. He stabbed at a fried shrimp on his plate and missed it twice before finally impaling it with the fork's silver prongs and popping it into his mouth. The chewing bought him an additional few seconds before he had to speak again.

He wiped sweat from his brow with his forearm and with a full mouth said, "Awfully hot in here."

Hayley was surprised when he had called her on her cell phone earlier in the day and asked if she was free for dinner that evening. Even if she hadn't been, she would have cleared her schedule because the suspense was killing her.

She had to know what was going on with him.

Was he going to break up with her or propose?

Whichever it was, she just wanted to know.

He swallowed the shrimp, set down his fork, and cleared his throat.

The dinner at West Street Café, near the waterfront, had up to this point been uneventful and filled with small talk. Nothing of consequence. But finally, near the end of the main course, there appeared to be a breakthrough.

He was about to get serious.

She downed the last of her glass of ice water to hydrate and prepare herself for what was about to come. Water was a poor substitute for her reliable Jack and Coke, but the restaurant was busy tonight and the bar was backed up.

"I'm listening."

"I've been thinking about us a lot lately and . . . Wait . . ." he said, reaching into the pocket of his tan khaki pants.

Was he about to pull out a ring?

He withdrew his hand from the pocket and there was a small white pill in the middle of his palm. He tossed it in his mouth and chased it by guzzling down some water.

He smiled weakly. "An antacid. I've been suffering from indigestion a lot lately. Probably because I've been eating tons of junk food and not your fine home cooking."

Smooth talker.

Just get to the point.

"Anyway . . ." he said, reaching over and taking her hand. "We've been together almost two years now and I believe it's time . . ."

"How dare you make an accusation like that?" a man's voice roared from across the room.

Hayley spun around in her seat just in time to see Olivia's husband, Nacho, spring to his feet and push the table aside with such force three wineglasses flew off and shattered into pieces on the floor.

"Chill, dude, don't be such a drama queen," Olivia's son, Red, said with a smirk, just before Nacho hauled him to his feet by the collar of his shirt. "Whoa, man, don't wrinkle the shirt."

"I loved your mother and only wanted the best for her! Not like you, who only came around when you needed something."

Peggy was at the table too and jumped to her feet, flushed with embarrassment, grabbing Nacho's arm. "Would you let him go? People are watching."

"He's insulting my honor!" Nacho shouted.

"Honor? What honor?" Red spit out, eyes narrowing. "Everyone knows why you married my mother. If it wasn't for her, you'd be back in Buenos Aires scheming and conning your way into whoever's bed so you'd have a roof over your head for the night."

"You smug little bastard! I will kill you!" Nacho yelled, punching Red in the nose with his hammy fist.

Red stumbled back, nose spurting blood, his eyes wide with shock. "You . . . you hit me. . . ."

Hayley glanced around for a waiter or the owner or someone to intervene, but everyone in the restaurant was slack jawed, in shock, watching the ugly scene unfold.

Peggy screamed. "Are you crazy? Red wants to

be an actor! How could you hit him in the face like that?"

"The only role he'll ever play is a lazy, no good, spoiled brat!" Nacho bellowed, gently rubbing his now throbbing fingers.

Finally, a young college-age waiter with slicked back hair and a scared look on his face intervened. "I'm sorry, but if you don't leave now, we're going to have to call the police."

Nacho nodded, turned to head for the door, but then Red bounced to his feet and came up behind him, wrapping an arm around his neck, trying to choke him.

"You're a fake and a cad and you never loved my mother! You just loved her money!"

Aaron had seen enough. He jumped up from the table, raced over, and tried pulling Red off Nacho. Red head butted him, catching him right in the face, and Aaron flew back into another table before sinking to the ground nursing an injured eye.

The owner rushed into the restaurant, having obviously been called by his staff and told of the emergency. He was apoplectic, screaming threats of arrests and lawsuits.

With the realization that their argument had spiraled way out of control, both Nacho and Red quickly calmed down. Nacho muttered apologies and bolted out the door. Red took the time to hand the owner a wad of cash for any damages and then, after stopping long enough to grab a napkin to hold over his bleeding nose, stormed out, dragging a still crying Peggy behind him.

Hayley was at Aaron's side in an instant. "Are you okay?"

"Yeah, a little humiliated about my fighting skills. Guess I won't be jumping in the ring with Floyd Mayweather Junior anytime soon."

"You were very brave."

The owner came over and knelt down next to them. "Dr. Palmer, should we get you a doctor to look you over?"

"Oh no, I'll be fine. Maybe just something for my eye."

The owner stood back up and grabbed the young waiter. "Quick. Go into the kitchen and get him a piece of steak," he said, before lowering his voice to continue. "Make sure it's one of the cheaper cuts."

The waiter was gone and back in a flash.

Hayley accepted the fleshy raw meat and helped Aaron carefully place it over his eye.

"Would you like me to call the police?" the owner asked Aaron.

"No. They both lost their temper and things just got overheated. It's a very trying time for both of them. I'm willing to let it go if you are."

The owner smiled, grateful the potentially litigious incident was over, and then, to insure the rest of the customers' dining experiences hadn't been completely ruined, generously offered every table free dessert. His gesture was met with resounding applause and lots of smiles.

Except for Hayley.

She wasn't smiling.

She knew if Aaron had been planning on proposing, he wasn't going to do it tonight.

Chapter 17

"I want you to drive straight home and take care of your eye," Hayley said, escorting Aaron to his parked car out in front of the West Street Café.

"I'm fine. It's just going to be a little black and blue for a few days. Get in. I'll drive you home."

"No. It's only a ten-minute walk to the house from here. I can use the exercise. I ate my entire Café Delight."

Café Delight was one of West Street Café's signature dishes, with lobster meat, North Atlantic shrimp, and mushrooms topped with a homemade cheese sauce, served over pasta. Sometimes she found herself dreaming about it at night.

"Okay, sorry we didn't get a chance to chat. Next time," Aaron said brusquely, jumping in his car and peeling away.

Chat?

That was all it was?

And boy, he sure didn't put up much of a fuss over driving her home.

Usually he was a lot more chivalrous, ever the

gentleman insisting it was his duty to see to it that she made it home safely.

Hayley scolded herself. Cut the poor guy some slack. He had just been popped in the eye by an obnoxious rich kid's head.

There were certainly better ways the evening could have ended for him.

She suddenly heard a noise off to her left near some parked cars. She spun around and spotted Nacho hunched over, quietly sobbing. She walked over to him and gently put a hand on his shoulder.

"I'm so sorry about everything, Nacho. I know this must be a very difficult time."

He nodded, wiping a finger across his nose and then blotting the tears running down his cheek with the sleeve of his jacket.

"I know what people think of me. I hear all the stories. But I loved her, Hayley. Truly I did. I loved Olivia deeply."

He was trying to convince her.

Desperate for someone to believe his intentions were honorable when he married a billionaire bacon heiress.

Hayley wasn't quite sold on that yet, but didn't let it show.

"All those people in the restaurant staring at me and judging me. Do you think they believed those terrible lies Red was shouting?"

"You shouldn't care what people think," Hayley said.

"You didn't answer me directly. That means you do."

"I don't know anything about you or your relationship with Olivia. I may have formed an opinion about her son and his girlfriend, but I'd rather not share it at this time. Now, why don't we go to my brother's bar and I'll buy you a drink? It looks like you could use one right about now."

"That sounds much better than spending the rest of the night licking my wounds," Nacho said, sniffling. "I'll drive."

"No. It's only a few blocks from here. Leave it here and we can walk."

They headed up the hill from the town pier along Main Street, veering left onto Cottage Street and arriving at Drinks Like A Fish in less than five minutes. The place was packed and there were no tables or stools at the bar available, so after picking up a Jack and Coke for herself and a vodka on the rocks for Nacho, the two of them retreated to the back near the dartboard. They huddled in a free corner where Nacho ranted for the next twenty minutes about how Red and Peggy were vultures and, if left to their own devices, would surely run Redmond Meats into the ground in less than a year. His whole face flared when he talked about Red, the wannabe actor with no clue how hard his mother had worked to keep the company in the black.

Nacho downed his vodka in one gulp and excused himself to go buy another one since Hayley had only taken a couple of sips of her cocktail and was hardly ready for a second round.

She noticed several women ogling Nacho as he waited to place his order with Randy, who was helping out his loyal bartender Michelle because the bar was so busy.

There was no denying it. Nacho was one fine

specimen of a man. And the whole Argentinean polo-playing backstory just added to his allure.

Wait until those local Maine girls on the prowl heard that one. There might be a stampede to talk to him.

One particularly drunk girl in formfitting jeans and a cream-colored sweater so tight she might as well have gone topless was all googly eyed and giggling as her friends pushed her forward, encouraging her to go talk to him.

Nacho was still patiently waiting at the bar for someone to take his order when she weaved her way through the crowd of fishermen, who had just stumbled through the door and were anxious to get mugs of beer in their hands. She slid in next to Nacho. She then casually turned and said something. He smiled politely at her before turning his attention away from her. She waited a few seconds and then leaned in and whispered something in his ear. Nacho shook his head, his smile a little tighter, and he spoke again. Randy suddenly appeared to serve him. The girl, crestfallen and embarrassed, scooted back to her friends, tail between her legs, having been resoundingly rejected.

When Hayley shifted her gaze back to Nacho she was surprised to see him beaming from ear to ear as he leaned forward to shout his order in Randy's ear above the noise in the bar. He also nimbly placed a hand over Randy's hand, which rested on the bar.

Randy was too busy to notice.

But Hayley did.

A few minutes later Nacho was back with two vodkas on the rocks.

"I did not want to have to wait in line again," he said before downing one and picking up the other.

He was loosened up real good now and talking nonstop. Several times he slipped into his native Spanish but caught himself and pivoted back to his second language, English. He kept one eye on the bar, watching Randy race back and forth as more customers poured in and placed their drink orders. Nacho was definitely not admiring Michelle, who was a stunning girl even with her hair pulled back and her face sweating from all the running around. The happy and by now inebriated fishermen all jock-eyed to flirt with her, but Nacho didn't pay her any mind.

He was too focused on Randy.

Hayley was sure of it.

One of the garbage bins overflowed from trash, so once the line for drinks dwindled, Randy seized the opportunity to secure the bag with a zip tie and carry it out back to the bin in the alley.

Nacho excused himself to go to the bathroom.

Hayley wasn't surprised when he walked right past the men's room and breezed directly out the back door.

She couldn't resist.

She had to follow him.

By the time she reached the door and stepped out into the alley, Randy was shoving Nacho away from him, the garbage bag dropped next to his feet.

"Buddy, I told you, I'm a married man," Randy said, trying hard to diffuse the situation without causing a scene.

Nacho came at him again. "Why are so many Americans obsessed with monogamy? Especially men. You know as well as I do the male species was not designed to sleep with just one person."

"Well, this one is, so let's just cool down, okay?" Randy said, pushing him back again, this time firmly enough for Nacho to get the message.

He put his hands up in surrender, swaying a little from side to side, clearly fuzzy from all the vodka, and then turned around to see Hayley watching the scene from the doorway.

That sobered him up a bit.

But just a bit.

"Stop looking at me like that," he slurred. "It doesn't mean anything. I'm just a little drunk. You want another drink?"

"No, I'm good," Hayley said as he pushed past her and stumbled back inside the bar.

Hayley turned to Randy, who deposited the plastic garbage bag in the bin and wiped his hands off.

"He just told me not even an hour ago how much he was in love with his wife," she said.

"Yeah, well, I'm sure he meant it. Like I love you. You're my sister. He probably loved Olivia the same way. Because, honey, if there's one thing we can be absolutely sure of at this point . . ."

"That man is an honest to goodness one hundred percent homosexual."

"Amen, sister."

Chapter 18

The rain pounded the windows and lightning flashed, illuminating the ornate staircase as Hayley helped Nacho up to the master bedroom at the Redmond Estate. He was still conscious but barely coherent, prattling on about what a Casanova he was back in the central Córdoba wine region where he grew up, a strapping young lad charming all the local daughters of the wine merchants. It was obvious he was desperately trying to cast doubt on Hayley's presumed assumption regarding his sexual orientation after spying him making unwanted advances toward her brother.

After Hayley and Randy had returned to the bar, Nacho was already enjoying another vodka on the rocks bought for him by a group of swooning college girls. He held court for nearly an hour, pawing them and stealing kisses in a blatant attempt to reassert his heterosexuality.

As successful as his efforts had been, especially with the girls, who were all quite smitten with the swarthy Latin lothario, for Hayley it had been honestly painful to watch.

Outside it had started to rain.

The roads would be slick driving home and visibility low, and Nacho at this point had been probably four times the legal limit, so there was no way she was going to allow him to drive himself home. At first he had resisted, but she had managed to snatch his keys away from him during last call, and with Randy's help, walked him back to his car at the restaurant and got him strapped into the passenger seat.

It had been a treacherous journey to Seal Harbor, but Hayley kept her eyes glued to the road. She could call for a taxi to get herself home once she got him back to the Redmond Estate. Nacho had spent the entire car ride with his face off to one side against the headrest, snoring.

She had to shake him awake when they arrived, and it took great effort to get him unstrapped and out of the car, but the wind and rain had finally seemed to arouse him and he started chattering again about life back in Córdoba and all his girlfriends and how American girls on television like the pretty young rich ones on *Gossip Girl* had inspired him to come to America and stake out his fortune.

By marrying one?

Hayley's neck ached by the time they had reached the king-size bed, and she gave Nacho a shove forward.

He had flopped face down on the bed and within four seconds was snoring again.

She turned him over and unbuttoned his shirt. He had abs to die for.

Then she got him out of his shoes and wriggled his pants off. The muscled legs of a star athlete.

She couldn't help but marvel at his flawless physique.

After placing his shoes by the bedside and folding his clothes and leaving them in a rocking chair by the window, she was about to snap off the light and close the door and call for a taxi home.

She stopped as Nacho started talking, his words slurred. He mumbled something about Red and Peggy telling him at dinner that they had checked in to a hotel in Bar Harbor because they refused to stay at the house as long as he was living there.

The servants had gone home for the night.

There was no one around to catch her if she did a little snooping. She started by searching the drawers of the night tables on each side of the bed.

Nothing of importance. Just some operating manuals for the television and stereo system. A compact hair dryer. Some receipts for a couple of meals in town.

She crossed to the closet and peered inside. There was a chain hanging from a light fixture on the ceiling of the closet. She yanked it and had to close her eyes, momentarily blinded by the high-wattage bulb. Once her vision readjusted she noticed all of the clothes belonged to Nacho.

A couple of suits. Lots of polo shirts in assorted bright colors. Some pressed shorts.

On the floor in the corner next to some very expensive-looking Gucci crocodile horse-bit loafers was a Nike gym bag. She knelt down, unzipped it, and rummaged through it.

She found a stack of used United Airlines tickets to exotic destinations around the world. An Argentine passport.

A birthday card from Olivia. She wrote lovingly about how her life had changed the day she met him. How his kindness gave her a new lease on life after years of a cold, distant father, an alcoholic, absent mother, and a long road littered with bad relationships with bad men ill-equipped to handle her immense wealth or too eager to exploit it. In Nacho, she had found her soul mate, her best friend, the man she knew in her heart would never betray her.

If only she could have seen him at the bar tonight hitting on Randy.

But then again, love wasn't always entwined with sex.

Hayley knew plenty of marriages where one of the spouses was closeted, but still loved their husband or wife.

She was definitely not one to judge any marriage, given how her own had ended in tatters.

There was another birthday card tucked in a side pocket. This one was still stuffed in its envelope, although it had been opened and she presumed read. She pulled the card out. On the cover was a lean, blond, devilish-looking stud in a bulging jockstrap and nothing else. Written on the top was, "The Best Gifts Come in Big Packages."

Hayley chuckled. Someone had a sense of humor.

She opened the card. Inside was printed "Happy Birthday."

Scrawled underneath that was the following message.

My dearest Nacho,
  You will always be my one and only Argentine side dish.
  I can't even count the ways you make me the happiest gringo on earth.
               My deepest love,
               Andy

Hayley flipped the envelope over to see the return address. It was a local residence, on Greeley Avenue. The name above the street number was Hawkins.

Andy.

Andy Hawkins.

Hayley knew exactly who that was. A young artist type in his midtwenties. He'd moved to the island as a child with his parents from out west. Arizona maybe.

He'd been an aspiring photographer. He had interned at the *Island Times* one summer when he was home from college, shooting pictures of the Fourth of July parade and the lobster festival and various band concerts in the village green. Now he was a freelancer working for both local papers whenever they needed an event photographed. If they both wanted him to cover the event, he'd go with the highest bidder.

Although they had never discussed it, Hayley always assumed he was gay.

Her instincts appeared to be right.

And apparently he was also the secret lover of Olivia Redmond's grieving husband.

Chapter 19

The man leapt from the creaky aluminum stands, jostling the other parents, and charged over to the college-age coach, wagging a finger in his face and shouting, "You need to put my son in left field now, before you throw the whole game!"

The fresh-faced coach, with big Obama-sized ears, stood toe to toe with the angry dad and held his ground. "Mr. Weston, I don't tell you how to run your bait shop. You don't get to tell me how to coach my kids."

The Little League game at the town ball field was already a nail biter. Tied score of four to four. Entering the ninth inning.

The other parents packed onto the shaky metal stands were all on edge, no matter which team they were there rooting for, because at this point it could go either way.

And one kid on the blue team was busy picking his nose and didn't see the ball roll right through his legs, allowing the red team to get two players on first and second base.

Tension was mounting.

The coach ordered the overzealous dad back to his seat.

The loud, brash father didn't budge.

It was basically a standoff.

The crowd exchanged disapproving looks.

His embarrassed wife scooted over to the dad and implored him to come with her and let the coach do his job.

Andy Hawkins recorded it all on his high-resolution camera.

"Aren't you here to record the game?" Hayley asked him as he snapped away, a big grin on his face.

"Yeah, that's what Sal's paying me for. But human drama like this is priceless. Besides, that's Ernie Weston. I ran into his wife at the Shop 'n Save last week and asked how she was doing and she hinted she might be leaving her husband, but needed proof of his boorish, unsportsmanlike behavior in case of a custody hearing."

"So you're going to sell her photos of him verbally abusing his son's Little League coach?"

"A guy's got to eat," Andy said, lowering his camera once Mrs. Weston finally managed to drag her still jeering husband back to the stands.

The game resumed.

One early developed, beefy kid who towered over his teammates furiously swung the bat, nearly cracking it, whacking the ball. It sailed high above the field and over the poor little guy in left field who desperately wanted to be left alone in peace to just pick his nose. By the time he managed to chase after it, scoop the ball up in his mitt, and throw it back to the third-base man, two boys in red had crossed home plate to the enthusiastic cheers of their parents.

The game was now six to four.

Angry dad blew his stack and stormed off to his car, much to the relief of his beleaguered wife, who glanced over at Andy to see how much of the tirade he'd gotten on camera.

Andy gave her an enthusiastic thumbs-up.

She waved happily and then chased after her husband, knowing she didn't have to scold him for his abhorrent behavior because it was definitely going to bite him in the ass eventually, during their divorce proceedings.

Andy aimed his camera at the kids in red still jumping up and down around their own coach, a heavyset, ponytailed woman in a cap and gray shirt and jeans.

"So, are you here to ask me about Nacho?" he asked, snapping more photos.

"How did you know?"

"I know *you*, Hayley. And the moment I got word that Olivia Redmond had been murdered, I expected you to turn up and pepper me with questions about my sordid affair with her bisexual husband."

"Am I that predictable?"

Andy lowered his camera again and smiled. "I would just say your reputation precedes you."

"Have you told the police?"

"They never asked me. I don't think they know about it yet. Nobody's come around to question me. But believe me, if that hot police chief shows up on my doorstep, I don't plan on hiding anything. And I do mean *anything*."

"So you don't consider your relationship with Nacho a secret?"

"I have no reason to keep it a secret," Andy said.

A *thwack* interrupted their conversation. The kid on the red team had hit another home run and their parents were going wild with lots of slaps on the back and big bear hugs.

The parents of the blue team remained seated with miserable, resigned looks on their faces.

Andy snapped what he could of the moment but still managed to miss most of it. He didn't seem too upset about it. He just shrugged and turned back to Hayley again. "Olivia knew about the two of us."

"Was she devastated when she found out?"

"Hell, no. She didn't care. Just as long as Nacho put on a good show for her high society friends and associates. She didn't like anyone knowing her business. But the truth was, Olivia and Nacho were more friends than lovers. They rarely had sex but they shared a much deeper bond. He really did adore her."

"But if he was scamming her for a green card and rich lifestyle, couldn't his adoration have just been an act?"

"Not a chance. The way I caught him looking at her, just the way he talked about her, there was no faking it. I was the one who was jealous because I knew I was always going to just be the boy on the side. I begged him to run away with me, but he refused. It wasn't about the money. He genuinely loved her and was never going to risk doing anything to hurt her."

Hayley was floored. But she had heard of such arrangements. Some of the most loving and long-lasting marriages she knew about never involved sex.

A roar from the crowd.

The red team had struck out and the blue team now had a chance to make up some runs to at least tie the game.

The nose picker in left field had miraculously caught the ball in his glove.

The rest of his team swarmed out to left field to raise him onto their shoulders and carry him back to the dugout.

The boy beamed with pride. So did his dad, nearly crying from relief that his son had managed to finally get some skin in the game.

And Andy had totally missed recording the kid's heroic catch for posterity.

"Listen, I'm going to leave you alone so you don't miss any more critical plays."

Andy smiled. "Let's hope the blue team doesn't score any hits, because I have to get over to the Harborside Hotel and cover a press conference."

"Press conference?"

"Yeah, your friend just flew into town."

"*My* friend?"

"Rhonda Franklin, host of *The Chat*, which I never miss, by the way. Shopping tips, arts, cooking, crafts, and celebrity interviews. What more could a self-respecting gay ask for?"

"She's *here*?"

"Yeah, she's making some kind of statement about Olivia Redmond's murder."

Chapter 20

Rhonda Franklin adjusted her dark sunglasses as she spoke, even though the sky was gray with a patchy cloud cover. Still, the flashes from the cameras belonging to the smattering of local and national press outside the Harborside Hotel were somewhat blinding, so hiding her eyes behind those oversized Christian Dior shades wasn't all for dramatic effect.

She straightened the dark blue jacket of her smart pantsuit that Hillary Clinton would be proud to wear and then clasped her hands together in front of her as she continued addressing the crowd of reporters. "Olivia Redmond was not just a celebrity friend. I have plenty of those. Actors or politicians with whom I've been photographed or served on a charity board so people assume we're best buddies who gab on the phone every day, but in reality we hardly know each other. No, Olivia was a *real* friend. A *true* friend. And we did talk on the phone every day. We gossiped, we laughed, we offered support to each other, a helping hand when needed. And now . . ."

Rhonda Franklin fished a white handkerchief

out of her pocket and wiped her nose as she valiantly fought back the inevitable onslaught of tears. "Now . . . she's gone. . . . No longer with us . . . And I have yet to face the fact that we'll never chat on the phone ever again."

"Chat" on the phone. She made sure to hit the word "chat." Emphasizing it above all the others.

The word seemed planted in her speech. It was an obvious yet subtle nod to Rhonda Franklin's TV show.

Which suggested she wasn't speaking 100 percent from the heart.

There was a little public relations cleanup happening at Rhonda Franklin's somber press conference.

"I knew you had a reason for changing our walking route," Mona said, rolling up the sleeves of her lobster red Bar Harbor sweatshirt and wiping the sweat off her brow. "You just wanted to see the circus."

Mona was right. Hayley had purposely veered left toward the town pier instead of right, which would have taken them in the direction of the park for their twice weekly power walk, because she didn't want to miss Rhonda's grief-stricken public appearance. She was curious to know what the TV star would say about her dearly departed friend.

Rhonda was putting on quite a performance.

She very slowly, very deliberately removed her glasses to reveal puffy eyes and very little makeup so her face looked even more drawn and dismayed. "It is my vow, my promise, to get to the bottom of this vicious, unspeakable crime. I will use every resource available to me to find out who is responsible for taking Rhonda away from us. I will not rest until the killer is brought to justice."

That would have been a powerful end to Rhonda's first public appearance since Olivia's death. Leave the reporters and go make good on her promise.

As if Rhonda was personally off to hunt down her best friend's murderer.

But Rhonda passed over the perfect exit.

She kept rambling.

"This has been the most difficult time of my life. Losing someone so dear to me. Who understands me. Whom I depended on. I will go on. I must go on. But my life's journey will be a bit lonelier now. . . ."

She did it.

Like most show biz personalities, with no publicity wrangler on the scene to stop her from talking, Rhonda had managed to make someone else's tragedy all about *her*.

Hayley had pushed her way far enough through the throng of reporters where she was able to slide in next to Andy Hawkins, who was snapping dozens of shots of the grieving superstar.

Rhonda was about to mercifully make her exit when she spotted Hayley in the crowd and waved at her. "Hayley! Hayley!"

The reporters all stared at Hayley, slack jawed that she had just commanded the attention of a major TV personality.

She gave Rhonda a quick wave back.

"Come inside and have a drink with me at the bar! Don't worry! Those jackals aren't allowed past the front door. We can have some privacy!"

Rhonda spun around on her heel and disappeared inside the hotel lobby.

Hayley turned to Mona. "You want to come?"

"No frigging way," Mona scoffed. "You go on without me. I'm underdressed and a sweaty mess."

"And I'm not? Come on. There's safety in numbers," Hayley said, grabbing a fistful of Mona's sweatshirt and dragging her through the group of reporters who parted and allowed them through where a bellhop had the door open for them.

"Welcome to the Harborside," he said with a tip of the hat.

Hayley and Mona found Rhonda already seated at the bar and downing a vodka martini with extra olives.

Hayley hugged Rhonda before sitting on the high back chair next to her. "I'm so sorry about Olivia."

"I'm still in a state of shock. I can't believe she's gone," Rhonda said, finishing her martini and pushing the glass toward the bartender, signaling him to bring her another round.

She swiveled her chair around to face Hayley and finally noticed Mona.

Her puffy red eyes instantly began to dance and flicker at the sight of the brawny woman in the stained red sweatshirt. "Who's your friend?"

"This is Mona. We were out power walking when we just by coincidence happened upon your press conference," Hayley fibbed.

"Such a pleasure to meet you," Rhonda said flirtatiously, reaching out to shake Mona's hand.

Mona grunted an incoherent reply before noticing Rhonda was waiting to take her hand. She grabbed it and pumped it a couple of times before letting it go.

Rhonda practically had to catch herself from falling off her bar chair because she was swooning.

"Your hands are so rough," Rhonda said, which was followed by a short giggle.

"That's because I haul lobster traps for a living," Mona said.

"Mona's being overly modest," Hayley said. "She owns her own business and supplies seafood to most of the restaurants on the island. She's very successful."

"I'm impressed," Rhonda said, eyeing Mona as if she were a rich, chocolatey dessert. "Can I buy you girls something to drink?"

"Beer's fine," Mona said with a shrug. "Nothing light or fussy. I want a dark ale."

The bartender nodded and turned to Hayley.

"I'll have what Ms. Franklin's having," Hayley said.

"It's Rhonda, please. We're friends now. There's no need to be formal."

"Okay, Rhonda."

"I'm only in town for a couple of days. I want to help Nacho with anything I can. How about I take you both out to dinner tonight? Are you free?"

"Sorry, I have a column due and I haven't even started writing it yet. I'm going to stay at home and be a hermit until I get it done," Hayley said.

Rhonda hardly blinked. Without missing a beat, she turned and stared at Mona. "What about you, honey? Would you like to have dinner with me?"

"You mean just the two of us? I don't even know you. God knows I don't watch your show. What would we talk about?"

"Oh, I'm sure we'll find some common ground if we give it the old college try."

"I didn't go to college."

"It was just a figure of speech, Mona," Hayley said, smiling.

"Guess I'd be a fool to turn down a free meal. You did say you are paying, right?"

"Absolutely."

"Good. You're the rich TV star!"

Rhonda erupted in a fit of giggles, so charmed by Mona's gruffness she could barely contain herself.

"My husband is home with the kids tonight, so I would love an excuse to stay out late for once," Mona said, suddenly wrapping her mind around this impromptu dinner date and starting to really warm to the idea.

"I'll do my best to keep you out as late as you want," Rhonda cooed. "As long as your husband doesn't mind."

"Who cares what he thinks? I deserve a night out! I call him 'the Slug' because he barely moves. You married, Rhonda?"

"No. I'm just a carefree single girl open to all possibilities."

"Smart choice! I hate men. All they know how to do is burp and fart and complain about everything. World would be a better place if it was just us girls, am I right?"

"You are so right, Mona!" Rhonda said. "Hayley, where have you been hiding this one?"

Hayley suppressed a smile. "Oh, there's no hiding Mona."

"So what fancy pants place are you taking me to tonight, Ron? You mind me calling you Ron?"

Rhonda Franklin shook her head vigorously. "You can call me whatever you want."

Chapter 21

The shrieking pierced the air with such intensity Hayley thought she had just punctured an eardrum.

The blond, curly haired, mop-topped toddler in pink corduroy coveralls ran across the room, clutching an iPhone in her tiny, pudgy fingers that were sticky from the maple syrup Hayley had served with the pancakes she had prepared for the kids' dinner.

On her heels was her exasperated older brother, around eight years old, yelling at her. "Give it back, Celia! Now!"

He chased her around the coffee table as she giggled and screamed before she stopped and dropped the phone in the glass of Pinot Grigio Liddy had just set down. Wine splashed on Liddy's lap and she jumped up with a start.

"For the love of God, look at what you've done, you obnoxious little rug rat!" Liddy barked at the precocious girl who wasn't the least bit affected by her stern and threatening demeanor. She just clapped her hands, amused at herself for soaking her brother's smart phone.

The discombobulated boy was on the verge of tears as he reached into Liddy's glass with his grubby, dirty little hands and carefully extracted his phone, wiping it off with his Spiderman T-shirt. "I'm going to kill you!"

"Hayley, please, you have to do something to wrangle these brats!" Liddy wailed as she marched into the kitchen to dump the rest of her wine into the sink and refill her glass.

Hayley had been trying to load Mona's dishwasher with the dirty dinner plates. Mona had asked her to come over and keep an eye on her kids while she was out to dinner with Rhonda Franklin since her deadbeat, couch potato husband, Dennis, would surely be parked in his usual man cave recliner watching TV and typically unengaged and uninterested in any required child rearing.

She had miraculously managed to talk Liddy into coming with her and keeping her company because sure enough, there was Dennis when they arrived, glued to one of those Vin Diesel *Fast and Furious* movies on cable. He'd barely acknowledged their presence.

"He's here in the room but basically an inanimate object," Liddy said.

Hayley valiantly tried to keep the kids entertained by whipping up batch after batch of blueberry pancakes, banana pancakes, pancakes with strawberry ice cream and whipped topping. The sugar rush was an unexpected side effect and she was now paying dearly for it. The older kids were upstairs locked in their rooms doing God only knew what, but the little ones demanded constant attention and were at present gleefully tearing the house apart. Probably like they did every night, which was why Mona rarely bothered cleaning.

Hayley knew she had to do something fast to get the situation under control.

A game. That would be fun.

"How about we play hide-and-seek? You go hide and then Aunt Liddy and I will try to find you!"

The blond moppet clapped her hands again and then scooted out of the room followed by her older brother and another six-year-old whose name Hayley could never remember. "You have two minutes and then I'm going to start looking for you!"

The room finally became quiet except for Vin Diesel's deep voice giving orders to his sexy team of race car drivers.

"This whole evening has been a nightmare!" Liddy said, gulping down her wine.

"Hey, I just bought us a few minutes of peace before they realize I'm never going to try and find them."

"Seriously, Dennis, are they like this every night?" Liddy asked.

His eyes were glazed over and he just stared at the flat screen TV as if in a trance.

"Did I ever tell you what a huge crush I had on you in high school, Dennis? I thought you were the sexiest man alive. I still do, in fact. If I didn't think Mona was going to walk through that door at any moment, I would rock your world," Liddy said.

Still nothing.

"I think if we set the house on fire, he wouldn't notice," Liddy said, shaking her head. "And for the record, Dennis, I was just trying to get a reaction out of you. I think you are the most disgusting, laziest human being in the whole world. How about that?"

His eyes didn't even blink. He just stared at the moving images on the screen.

"I've seen more life in a coma patient," Liddy said before noticing a pair of headlights outside the living room window as a car pulled into the driveway. "Mona's home!"

Hayley and Liddy ran to stare out the window at the car.

"They're just sitting there. What do you suppose they're saying?"

"Probably good night."

An agonizingly long three minutes passed before Mona finally got out of the car and Rhonda Franklin drove away.

Mona trudged through the door and shook off her coat.

"Well, how did it go?" Hayley asked, running over to greet her.

"Okay, I guess. She spent the whole night telling me how attractive I was, how charming I was, how interesting I was. I have to say, it was nice hearing some compliments for a change. Dennis hasn't said anything nice about me since . . . Scratch that. Dennis has never said anything nice to me. Even when he proposed to me, he just said, 'I might as well make an honest woman out of you because nobody else will likely man up and do it.' That's a direct quote!"

"I'm sure Dennis shows you how he feels just by loving you," Hayley said.

"Yeah. And I wish he'd stop it. I'm tired of getting pregnant all the time."

"So Rhonda Franklin has a crush on you. That is so sweet," Hayley said, smiling.

"Pretty much. Which is kind of weird. Don't get me wrong, I'm flattered. But why would she automatically think I'm a lesbian?"

Hayley kept her lips sealed.

The polite thing to do was just to avoid answering the question.

Liddy had just finished a bottle of Pinot Grigio, so she wasn't so concerned with proper social etiquette. "You can't be serious."

"No, I'm being very serious. Do I come off as gay?"

"Mona, at the risk of sounding blunt . . ."

"Here we go . . ." Hayley sighed.

"You are the walking picture of a card-carrying lesbian."

"I am?"

"Oh, honey, your lack of self-awareness is adorable; am I right, Hayley?"

"I am so not getting involved in this conversation," Hayley said.

Neither was Dennis.

He actually moved. He reached for the TV remote and turned up the volume in an attempt to drown their voices out.

"But I've been married to Dennis for twenty years," Mona said, confused.

"A lot of lesbians are trapped in loveless marriages. Now that society is more accepting, they are finally able to ditch the deadweight—and yes, I'm looking at you, Dennis—and finally become who they really are."

"But you're forgetting one thing. If George Clooney was to walk in this room right now I'd jump his bones faster than a fruit fly on a skirt steak," Mona said.

She certainly could paint a picture.

"I'm not saying you're actually *gay*, Mona. You just look the part. Right, Hayley?"

"Stop trying to drag me into this. I'm not participating in your offensive stereotyping," Hayley said, picking up a few plastic toys that had been strewn around the room by Mona's high energy brood.

"Well, I for one think it's cute that Rhonda is a little infatuated with our Mona."

"I think she's a little more than just infatuated. She told me she loved me," Mona said, crossing to the kitchen and grabbing a bottle of Bud Light out of the fridge.

"She said what?" Hayley screamed, no longer able to refrain from the conversation.

"She loves me," Mona said, popping the cap off and guzzling down half the bottle. "Is that so hard to believe?"

"Well, that's just . . . how could she . . . I mean . . ." Liddy sputtered, a disbelieving look on her face. "That's just . . . insulting. It's downright insulting."

"What do you mean insulting?" Hayley wanted to know.

"Being infatuated with Mona's, how shall I say, unique personality is one thing, but *love* her? That's ridiculous. Rhonda Franklin is rich and famous and can have anyone she wants, and if she is going to come to Bar Harbor and fall in love, well, it should be with someone like *me*!"

"*You*?" Hayley asked, floored.

"Yes, me. We met in New York briefly after the show taping. I'm a successful businesswoman. I dress well. I can engage in scintillating conversation. I'm the real deal. A true catch. It would make much more sense for Rhonda to fall for someone like me!"

"You're bananas, you know that?" Hayley said, mouth agape. "You're not even remotely gay."

"That may be true. But I'm a woman of many tastes. I've traveled. I'm worldly. I could be mistaken for gay. A lip gloss lesbian."

"Lip*stick* lesbian," Hayley said, laughing.

"Whatever. I think Rhonda just needs to spend time with me and then she'll see that I'm much more cultured and worthy of her love than Mona."

"Liddy, would you please stop? You're acting crazy and you're starting to scare me. Now, Mona, did she mention Olivia at all during your dinner?"

"Yeah. A few times. She was saying the right things. How she missed her. How they were very close. But I had the feeling she was hiding something."

"What?"

"I'm not sure. She mentioned at one point they had a fight, but then she quickly changed the subject. And at another point, around the time dessert came, she slipped and said something about how guilty she felt."

"Guilty? Why would Rhonda feel guilty?"

"I don't know. But I got the distinct feeling something bad went down between them."

"Did she give any indication what it was?"

"No. She seemed to catch herself, like she clearly didn't want to talk about it, and then she went right on to something else. I think it was how the flame from the candle on the table made my eyes dance."

"Oh brother!" Liddy howled.

Rhonda's recent press conference was obviously a way for her to promote the idea that she and Olivia had been the best of friends. But if in reality there had been a wedge between them, then Hayley was going to find out what it was that had driven them apart.

Island Food & Spirits
by
Hayley Powell

It's been unusually busy at the *Island Times* newspaper office with everyone gearing up for what appears to be another tourist season. As office manager, I've been inundated with phone calls from summer businesses placing ads, press releases about upcoming events, and out of state customers requesting address changes to their summer residences on our beautiful island. These high maintenance readers hit the roof if they miss one issue of the paper because it was sent to the wrong address. This is serious business as far as they are concerned, and it's my job to make sure the switch over goes smoothly and irate calls to complain are kept to a minimum.

After an exhausting day fielding an avalanche of calls, I was nearly home free. It was three minutes to five. Almost quitting time. Since I think about food about 90 percent of the time, I was focused on going home and whipping up a simple supper of my Apple Bacon Egg Bake. After calming my nerves with a cocktail or two, of course. I knew in my gut I had been indulging in bacon a little too much lately, but with both my kids out of town, it was easy to make a package last longer without a pair of ravenous teens in the house. I didn't have to share any, which is a bonus for me but not my waistline.

I was halfway out the door when the phone rang. Part of me desperately wanted to ignore it and just breeze out the door to freedom. But the responsible voice inside me argued I should answer it. I sighed, turned around, and walked back to the desk, scooping up the receiver.

"Good afternoon, *Island Times*. This is—"

That's all I managed to get out.

I just heard screaming.

It was a woman. That much I could make out. But I had no idea what she was saying. Her voice was high and shrill and unintelligible.

And angry.

Boy, was she angry.

I tried several times to interject and

attempt to calm her down, but she was having none of it.

After a few minutes, once my ears had adjusted to the screaming voice, I was able to make out the gist of what had riled her up so much.

Apparently this poor woman recently had a run-in with our local law enforcement and her name appeared in our Police Beat column, a weekly feature that is read religiously by everyone because it meticulously details all the recent arrests and does not withhold any names. It's like our small town version of TMZ, a must-read for gossip lovers.

Well, this woman was appalled that her name was highlighted in bold for a crime she swore she did not commit. Something about being arrested for indecent exposure after drinking too much red wine and wandering out into the street naked looking for her dog, who got out the back door. She continued without taking a breath, ranting about being innocent until proven guilty in a court of law, and how the paper printing this filthy piece of trash would sully her good name in town!

I tried to explain that our editor, Sal Moretti, was out of the office, and I would be happy to take a message and have him call her back, but she wasn't interested in anything I had to say. She preferred to rail against muckraking journalism and her besmirched reputation and the lawsuit she would certainly file against the *Island Times* for this abhorrent breach of journalistic ethics.

Apple Bacon Egg Bake.

Apple Bacon Egg Bake.

I tried focusing on something to look forward to once this phone conversation was mercifully at an end.

Finally, after what seemed like an hour, but was only around six minutes, she stopped talking, took a long breath, and then started in again. She was demanding a correction since our reporters were obvious morons incapable of getting any facts right.

In fact, she told me, they didn't even spell her name correctly.

"My name is Suzette Smith!" she howled. "You idiots said I was Susan Smith!"

She then demanded that we fix the mistake immediately and said she wanted to see the correction in the next issue of the newspaper or she would take serious action against us.

I just stood there slack jawed, the phone pressed to my ear. This woman was so mad she didn't even realize what she was doing. There were dozens of Smiths on the island. I tried to explain that our mistake might work in her favor, but if we corrected it, then everyone would know exactly who the naked drunk woman was. But she cut me off in midsentence and said she had heard enough from me.

"Just make the correction!"

So in the sweetest voice I could muster, I told her not to worry. I would type it up myself and personally make sure it was in the next edition of the *Island Times* newspaper.

Suzette Smith.

Then she slammed the phone down in my ear.

After triple checking the exact spelling of her name, with a smile I e-mailed it off to the Police Beat editor. It was all about customer satisfaction. I figured once she calmed down and reviewed our conversation over again in her mind, she might realize she should have left the matter well enough alone. But by then, I would be home chowing down on my delicious Apple Bacon Egg Bake.

I love having breakfast for dinner, especially since I'm always running late in the morning and only have time for a dry piece of toast, so this is a decadent indulgence that has to be accompanied by a Bloody Mary, with a crisp bacon garnish, of course!

Bloody Mary with a Bacon Garnish

Ingredients
1½ ounce vodka
3 ounces tomato juice
½ teaspoon Worcestershire sauce
3 teaspoons or more (if you like hot)
   Tabasco sauce
½ teaspoon celery salt
½ tablespoon horseradish sauce
Salt and pepper to taste
1 cooked crispy slice of bacon for
   garnish (optional)

Fill a glass with ice. Stir together all of the ingredients in another glass, except the bacon. Pour stirred ingredients into the glass filled with ice, garnish with bacon, and enjoy!

This bacon egg dish is a two-serving recipe, which is perfect for a portion tonight and another tomorrow morning. What a great change it will be from my morning toast!

Apple Bacon Egg Bake

Ingredients
3 eggs
1 small apple diced
1 cup frozen hash browns thawed
⅓ cup of milk

⅓ cup sour cream
⅓ cup shredded cheddar cheese (or your favorite)
3 strips of bacon cooked and crumbled
Salt and pepper to taste

In a small bowl, beat the eggs. Stir in the apple, hash browns, milk, sour cream, three tablespoons cheese, one tablespoon crumbled bacon, salt and pepper.

Pour mixture into two 2-cup baking dishes or a small casserole dish sprayed with cooking spray. Top each with the rest of the cheese and bacon.

Bake in a preheated oven at 350 degrees for 35 to 40 minutes or until knife inserted in center comes out clean.

Pour yourself another Bloody Mary and this is what breakfast for supper is all about!

Chapter 22

Hayley could make out the body from behind the yellow police tape that was tied between two trees deep in the woods of Acadia National Park, outside town. The body was crumpled and twisted around, but the head was turned in her direction and she knew from the pictures in the *Island Times* that it was definitely Dr. Alvin Foley, the scientist from the Jackson Lab who had been missing for weeks.

It had been a quiet morning at the paper before word quickly spread that a hiker, who'd wandered off the path into the woods just after sunrise, had stumbled across a dead body.

Bruce had flown out of his office and asked Hayley if she wanted to tag along with him. She knew the only reason he wanted her to come with him was because the police chief was her brother-in-law and he might be more willing to share key details of the investigation if Hayley was the one asking the questions.

Hayley knew her presence would make absolutely no difference. Sergio was a professional. And helping her colleague Bruce Linney write a story would be the last thing on his mind.

The cops had cordoned off the area and they were a safe distance from where the investigators were hard at work examining the scene for evidence.

"That's him. That's Dr. Foley, for sure. What's he doing all the way out here?" Bruce said, more to himself than to Hayley, who was standing next to him.

"Maybe he fell while jogging and hurt himself and didn't have a cell phone to call for help," Hayley offered, not quite convinced of her own theory.

"I heard one of the cops say he was shot," a reporter from the *Bar Harbor Herald* said, angling his way to the front of the small crowd of spectators who had heard the news on their police scanners at home and rushed to the scene. "Bullet hole straight through his chest."

"So we're talking homicide," Bruce said, staring at the body.

"Nothing's been confirmed. Just what I heard," the reporter said.

Bruce nodded, then turned to Hayley. "Maybe he was murdered somewhere else, like in his home, or closer to town, and the killer drove out here and dumped the body off the beaten path hoping it wouldn't be found."

"This means there have been two local murders in less than a month. First, Dr. Foley, and then Olivia Redmond," Hayley said, her whole body shivering at the thought of a serial killer on the loose in Bar Harbor.

"I sure would love to get the chance to talk to the chief for a few minutes," Bruce said, eyeing Hayley.

"Not going to happen, Bruce. He won't talk to me. Not right now anyway. And I don't want to interfere with his job."

One of the investigators covered Dr. Foley's body with a white sheet as a few others began packing up their equipment.

"Looks like they're wrapping up. We might as well head back to the office," Bruce said, sighing, frustrated.

As they trudged back to Bruce's car, parked on the roadside, Bruce gently placed a hand on Hayley's shoulder. "I have a proposition for you."

"What kind of proposition?" Hayley asked, drawing a sharp intake of breath, not entirely sure she wanted to hear his answer.

"I want you to cowrite this story with me."

This was not what she was expecting.

"You mean work together?"

"Yes. I know we've butted heads in the past and I haven't always treated you with respect, and I'm sorry for that. I think part of the reason for that is because sometimes I feel threatened by you."

Well, this certainly was a surprise.

Bruce was actually having a Come to Jesus moment.

"You may just write a cooking column, but you're also whip smart and a damn good investigative journalist in your own right."

"Bruce, I don't know what to say. . . ."

"Let me finish. I'd be an idiot if I kept trying to pretend you're not my equal. I've spent a hell of a lot of time trying to show you up and put you in your place, and I've screwed it up every time. I'm surprised Sal still keeps me around. He should just give the crime column to you and let you do double duty."

"I don't know what to say. . . ."

"Say yes. And I'm not pushing for this because you have an in with the police chief and I want to take advantage of that."

Hayley crossed her arms and raised an eyebrow at him.

"Okay. That may be a small part of why I want to team up."

"Why all of a sudden the change of heart? Why now?"

Bruce shrugged. "Beats me. Maybe it's the old saying, 'If you can't beat 'em, join 'em.'"

There was a long pause.

"Or maybe I just want to spend more time with you. . . ."

He let the words drift off.

At first she thought she had heard wrong. Spend more time with her? That was the last thing she ever thought Bruce Linney would want.

"So what do you say?"

"I'm flattered, Bruce. Truly I am. But I'm going to have to say no. I'm afraid we'd wind up killing each other. We have such different approaches. Don't get me wrong, I admire your writing and your sense of justice, really I do—"

"You can stop. I get it."

"It's just that—"

"Seriously, Hayley. Drop it. It was just a thought I decided to throw out there. It's no big deal."

"I appreciate the offer though. Maybe another time. . . ."

Bruce smiled and nodded and then got into the car.

Hayley jumped into the passenger seat.

They drove back to town in silence.

Had she reacted too swiftly? He had just taken her by surprise. She had no idea where all this was coming from.

Bruce had never shown an ounce of interest in her as a crime reporter let alone as the paper's office manager and cooking columnist.

Now he wanted to team up like the characters in her favorite TV shows she watched religiously when she was a kid, such as *Remington Steele, Moonlighting,* and *Scarecrow and Mrs. King*.

But what all those shows had in common was an obvious sexual tension.

And the thought of sexual tension with Bruce Linney was utterly ridiculous.

She had been repulsed by him ever since the two ill-fated days they had dated in high school. Awkwardly asking her out in front of her locker. The movie date in Ellsworth where they sucked face in the back row during a Saturday night showing of *The Brady Bunch Movie*. Catching him eyeing the pretty blonde in front of them while still making out with her. It was awful. And mercifully short. By Monday they were both using their friends to get the word out to everyone that they were totally uninterested in repeating such an obvious mistake. That was the end of any romantic notions she'd had about Bruce Linney.

And she didn't see her feelings changing anytime soon.

She glanced over at Bruce, who gripped the wheel, staring straight ahead, his face void of emotion except for a slight grimace.

The chirping of Hayley's cell phone disrupted the

tension and she was grateful for the call. It was from Mona.

"Hey, what's up?"

"Rhonda and I just had lunch."

"How nice. Are you calling to tell me she proposed?"

"Oh, that's cute, Hayley. You can make all the jokes you want, but we're just friends. I'd be a fool to turn down all these free meals and time away from my kids!"

"I'm happy for you, Mona."

"Our relationship is completely innocent. Although she did try and play footsies with me under the table at dinner the other night. I jumped up and accidentally knocked our table over because I thought it was a friggin' rat crawling up my leg. I had to shell out a few bucks for some broken plates and wineglasses. But Rhonda and I had a good laugh about it on the way home."

"We're almost back at the office, Mona, so I'm going to have to go soon. Was there anything else?"

"Of course there's something else! Do you think I'm just calling to brag about my new BFF who is a big Hollywood star? I'm calling to tell you that when I dropped Rhonda off at her hotel after lunch, she forgot her bag in my car, so I took it up to her room to return it, and that's when I spotted that floozy dating Olivia Redmond's son sneaking into some other guy's room, and the two of them looked pretty cozy. She was kissing him and slobbering all over his face. When she saw me looking, she turned away and covered her face and they hightailed it inside his room and slammed the door.

"Did you get a good look at the man she was with?"

"Older guy. Nice looking. Well dressed. And he had an accent."

"What kind of accent?"

"I don't know. He sounded a lot like that guy in the last James Bond movie who played the bad guy, Blowhard."

"Blofeld. Christoph Waltz."

"Yeah, him."

Christoph Waltz, the Oscar-winning Austrian actor.

He speaks German.

Thorsten Brandt.

Peggy was with Thorsten Brandt.

The Redmond Meats executive whom Hayley had seen arguing with Olivia the day before someone snapped her neck in the garden.

Chapter 23

Wildwood Stables in Acadia National Park offered a variety of horse-drawn carriage rides from mid-June through early October, but many of the wealthier residents who lived on the island during the summer season were given the option of bringing their own horses for riding on the carriage roads. They were allowed to rent stables in the horse camp provided on the property, situated on the southeast end of the island near Seal Harbor.

Hayley had followed Thorsten Brandt from the Harborside Hotel, in town, to the Wildwood Stables, tailing him in her car along the two-way section of the Park Loop Road going south past Bubble Pond and Jordan Pond House. She pulled into an empty space in the parking lot adjacent to the stables and watched Thorsten, dressed in a tight-fitting lime green polo shirt and white pants and riding boots, as he flagged down the stable boy to bring around his horse.

The young stable boy trotted off to fetch Thorsten's

horse, which he called Thunder. Hayley got out of her car and walked across the yard, finding cover among some trees lining the property. She watched curiously as Thorsten waited until he was alone before pulling his cell phone out of his back pocket and pressing a button to make a call.

A few seconds later Thorsten was whispering intensely into the phone.

Although there was a slight breeze that made eavesdropping somewhat of a challenge, Hayley managed to make out most of the one-sided conversation.

"Try to be patient, Peggy. It's all going to work out as planned. I promise you," he said, glancing around to make sure he was alone, not noticing Hayley hiding behind the trees a few feet away from him.

Peggy.

The *Downton Abbey*-loving girlfriend of Olivia's son, Red.

And probably the secret lover of Olivia's right-hand man.

"I know. But don't worry about Red. His head is up in the clouds. He has no idea what's going on. The kid has zero interest in running his mother's company anyway. He's a vegetarian! Why would he want to have anything to do with a bacon company? Trust me, darling. I'm confident we can strong-arm him into voting my way, and then it's done. I will have full control of the company and then we can—"

Peggy apparently cut him off.

He just stood there listening, his cell phone clamped to his ear, an annoyed look on his face.

"I understand. Stop worrying. I've got this covered. The kid will never know what hit him."

The stable boy arrived, leading a horse by a long leather rein.

"I've got to go now. Just sit tight. It will all work out in our favor," Thorsten said, ending the call and stuffing the phone in his back pocket.

"Excuse me!" a shrill voice said, piercing the air, surprising Hayley, who spun around to find a family of tourists, the mother thrusting a digital camera in her face. "Would you be so kind as to take our picture?"

They were all beaming from ear to ear. The mother. The father. And two moppets. One boy. One girl. The perfect midwestern family.

It was unusual for tourists to show up on the island in the spring. They mostly arrived during the summer months. But these early birds were here, and they had no idea they were causing enough of a scene to expose Hayley's hiding place.

"Yes, I'd . . . I'd be happy to," Hayley said softly, taking the camera from the mother as the family lined up in a row and threw their arms around each other.

Hayley glanced back to see Thorsten staring at her, suddenly aware of her presence. He turned to the stable boy and spoke quietly in his ear. The boy ran off toward the stables.

Hayley snapped a photo of the family. The mother immediately snatched the camera from her and inspected the photo.

She frowned. "It's too dark. We need to use the flash. Would you mind taking another one?"

Left with no choice, Hayley smiled and nodded and tried again.

The mother grabbed the camera out of her hands

once more and examined the photo. This time she was satisfied. After a perfunctory "thank you," the family wandered away and Hayley was left alone.

Thorsten casually approached her. "Ms. Powell, right? The cooking columnist."

Hayley feigned surprise. "Yes, I am. You're . . . ?"

"Thorsten Brandt. I'm on the Board of Directors for Redmond Meats. We met at the estate not too long ago. Before . . ."

"Yes, of course. I remember. How are you, Mr. Brandt?"

"Fine. I didn't know you ride."

Hayley smiled tightly. "Yes. I love riding. Horses are my life."

Really? Horses were her life?

Okay, that was a slight exaggeration. Yes, she'd ridden a lot when she was a kid and loved watching reruns of *The Big Valley* with Barbara Stanwyck, Linda Evans, and Lee Majors on the local retro TV channel, but that was about the extent of her experience with horses.

But she needed an explanation for why she was at the Wildwood Stables, and a love of horses was the first thing that popped into her mind.

"Really?" Thorsten said, letting the word roll off his tongue slowly enough to make the point that he hardly believed her.

"Yes," Hayley said, doubling down.

The stable boy returned with another horse, at the behest of Mr. Brandt, and was having trouble controlling him. He gripped the leash, but the horse was skittish and uneasy and bucked and resisted the reins.

"Well, since you are an experienced rider, would

you like to join me for a jaunt along the carriage trails?"

"Oh, thank you, but no, I wasn't planning on—"

"Please. I'd love the company," Thorsten said, eyes boring into her, challenging her, daring her to back down and admit she was lying.

"Sounds lovely," Hayley heard herself saying.

What was she thinking? Thorsten Brandt was an arrogant snob. She detested that kind of privileged sense of superiority.

She knew to beware of men like him. And yet she had just played right into his hand.

But maybe a pleasant horse ride along the carriage trails might be the perfect opportunity to grill him and get him to slip up and say something he shouldn't about any knowledge he might have regarding Olivia's grisly murder.

Thorsten signaled the stable boy to bring the horse he was desperately trying to keep under control over to Hayley. Then Thorsten casually walked over and petted the horse from the other side, adjusting the saddle to make sure it was tight enough.

"This is Lightning. The brother of my horse Thunder," Thorsten said with a smirk. "He can be a bit defiant on occasion, but I'm sure an experienced rider such as yourself can handle him."

He locked eyes with Hayley, waiting for her to back down.

The smug smile made her bristle. There was no way she was going to let this self-satisfied SOB get the best of her.

"He's beautiful. I'd be honored to ride such a magnificent horse."

Did she really just say that?

Had she just signed her own death warrant?

The horse was obviously agitated and jerked fitfully as the stable boy brushed his mane with his hand, trying to calm him down.

Hayley's anger at Thorsten's obvious disdain and sexist attitude outweighed her common sense and she took the reins as if she was outside her body, watching the scene unfold, helpless to stop what was sure to come.

Thorsten knew she had been following him.

He knew she probably suspected he might be somehow connected to Olivia's murder.

But his cool, calculated demeanor never wavered. He just smiled, calm and relaxed as he watched the stable boy grip the reins.

Hayley took a deep breath and mounted the horse.

She could do this.

She had ridden lots of horses when she was younger.

It was just a matter of exerting control over the animal.

Her butt had barely touched the contours of the brown leather saddle before Lightning reared up in a panic and shot off down the carriage trail.

Hayley grabbed the reins, desperately trying to slow him down, but he was obviously spooked by something and there was no stopping him. She bounced up and down as the frightened horse galloped along the dirt path with no intention of stopping.

"Whoa, Lightning! Whoa!"

But her commands fell on deaf ears.

This horse was not going to listen.

She contemplated jumping. But the horse was running so fast now she knew it would be impossible for her to land without at least a few broken bones.

She just held on to the reins with all her might and hoped for the best.

Lightning neighed and kept galloping—dust from the dirt path kicking up like a cloud cover—before veering off into a wooded area toward a pond.

When they reached the edge of the pond, the horse seized up, stopping abruptly, and Hayley found herself thrown out of the saddle and sailing through the air before splashing down in the pond face first. Her nose and mouth filled with water, and for a brief second she felt as if she was drowning before flapping her arms and emerging above the surface, sputtering and coughing and finally able to find some footing.

Lightning was a few feet away, calmly grazing on some grass, oblivious to the fact he had just nearly killed her.

Hayley dragged herself out of the pond, picking weeds from her hair and spitting out pond scum as she crawled over to a dry patch of land spotted with sweet white violets.

She wiped her mouth.

She heard the sound of horse hooves trotting up the carriage trail in her direction and lifted her head to see Thorsten Brandt, confidently astride his loyal horse Thunder, approaching.

"Are you all right?" Thorsten said, unsuccessful in his attempt to pretend he wasn't thoroughly enjoying this moment.

"Yes, I'm fine," Hayley said defiantly, climbing to

her feet and brushing off the dirt. "I can't imagine what could have spooked him so much."

Thorsten shrugged. "He usually responds to an experienced rider."

He was calling her on her lie.

He knew she wasn't experienced.

He was teaching her a lesson.

"Perhaps Lightning has a sixth sense. Most animals do," Thorsten said, his superior German accent dripping in judgment.

"About what?"

"They know on some level when someone is lying, when someone is not being upfront and honest."

"I really don't know what you mean."

Thorsten ran his hand down the black mane of his steed Thunder, and then casually and quietly said, "It might be in your best interest to stop lying about your intentions and stop poking your nose in private matters that don't concern you. You obviously can't handle Lightening so I would suggest you walk him back to the stables."

And with that, Thorsten slapped the reins against Thunder's back and the horse shot off down the carriage trail, leaving Hayley soaked and shivering and utterly humiliated.

After four attempts at grabbing Lightning's reins, Hayley finally managed to get a good grip on the leather strap, and then she walked the rebellious and unruly horse back to the Wildwood Stables.

She was more than happy to hand him off to the stable boy, who offered his sincere apologies.

She thanked him and was about to hobble back to her car, still sore from being shot like a cannonball into the pond, when she heard the stable boy gasp.

"How did this get here?"

She turned around. "What?"

"There's a burr in his saddle."

Hayley walked over and the stable boy held out a prickly round object.

A burr.

Planted right underneath Lightning's saddle.

"No wonder he was so unruly. The second you mounted him he felt a sharp jolt of pain."

"How did it get there?"

The stable boy shook his head, a perplexed look on his face. "I don't know. I put his saddle on myself before I brought him out. I swear it wasn't there."

Hayley didn't have to press him any further because she knew how it got there.

Thorsten Brandt.

He'd slipped it under the saddle right before Hayley mounted Lightning.

She was sure of it.

He was hell-bent on teaching Hayley a lesson.

Or worse.

He was trying to kill her.

Chapter 24

"This is the tastiest spaghetti carbonara I've ever had in my life," Aaron said, twirling the pasta around his fork and shoveling it into his mouth. "What's your secret?"

"I'm just very generous with the parmesan and bacon," Hayley said. "Seriously. It's one of the easiest dishes to make."

She lifted the bottle of Chardonnay and refilled his glass and then handed him a plate with a lone piece of crispy garlic bread.

He waved it away. "No, thanks. I'm getting full and I don't want to leave anything on my plate. I want to wipe it clean."

There was no danger of that not happening. There were just a few strands of spaghetti and some bacon bits left on it.

Hayley had been surprised when Aaron had called her as she drove home from the stables and told her he was free for dinner.

It was very last minute and he suggested they go out, but Hayley was in the mood to cook for him, and she preferred spending time with him alone at home instead of in a crowded restaurant where they would barely hear each other above the din of the other diners.

She also wanted him relaxed, in a quiet environment, where he might feel comfortable getting off his chest whatever it was that was on his mind.

Aaron set his fork down. "That's it. No more. It was delicious, Hayley."

"Thank you. Why don't you go into the living room and I'll bring in dessert and coffee and we can have a chat," she said, starting to clear the table.

"About what?" he asked curiously.

"Whatever it is you want to talk about."

They had made it through the whole dinner just making small talk. How busy his vet practice had gotten. How he was thinking about bringing in a partner to help alleviate the workload. A little about her appearance on *The Chat* and what a lovely time she had in New York.

A bit about how the kids were doing in their various exciting endeavors, but how she missed them and looked forward to Dustin coming home and Gemma visiting during her next college break.

Aaron seemed to be consciously avoiding what he had begun to say at the restaurant before he was interrupted by Nacho and Red's violent brawl.

She didn't want to pressure him, but she also couldn't take the suspense for much longer.

She had to know.

Her life seemed to be on hold, just waiting for him to work up the courage.

Aaron sighed, wiped the sides of his mouth with

a cloth napkin, and set it down on the table. "Okay. I wasn't expecting to do this tonight. I'm not prepared. But I guess now is as good a time as any."

The doorbell rang.

"You've got to be kidding me," Hayley groaned.

"Saved by the bell," Aaron said with a smile.

And he obviously meant it.

Hayley wagged a finger at him. "You're not off the hook. I'm getting rid of whoever that is."

"I'll go make the coffee," Aaron said, standing up, a relieved look on his face. He quickly made his escape into the kitchen.

Frustrated, Hayley marched to the front door. She had to slow down halfway there. Her muscles ached and her back was still sore from the fall off the horse earlier that day. She was going to be in pain for some time.

When she reached the door, she flung it open to discover Mona standing on the porch.

At least it looked like Mona.

The woman in front of Hayley was much better dressed. She wore a lavender cashmere sweater and black pants and had a pearl necklace around her neck. If not for the pageboy haircut and the permanent scowl, Hayley might not have recognized her.

"Mona, what on earth . . . ?"

"What? Have I got something on my face?"

"No . . . you look . . . nice."

"Thank you."

"And what's that scent? Are you wearing . . . perfume?"

"Yeah. It's Beyoncé Heat. My daughter had some

in her room she let me borrow. Smells nice, huh? So are you going to let me come in or what?"

The rehearsed speech Hayley had mentally prepared on her way to answer the door about how this was a bad time was completely lost. She was too stunned by Mona's sharp and attractive appearance to object as her friend pushed her way inside.

"You busy?" Mona said, looking around, noticing the dirty dinner plates Hayley had set back down on the table and the two half-empty wineglasses.

"Kind of. Aaron's here and we were just about to—"

Aaron walked in from the kitchen with two piping hot cups of coffee.

"Oh, hi, Aaron. Thanks," Mona said, snatching one of the cups out of his hands so aggressively some coffee almost splashed all over his shirt.

"You're welcome. Good to see you, Mona," Aaron said.

Of course it was good to see her.

Her arrival was the perfect excuse to avoid proposing to Hayley.

Or dumping her.

At this stage, it was a fifty-fifty chance of going either way.

"Yeah, Aaron. Been a long time. Hayley tells me you've been in hiding. She never sees you. Makes us all wonder what the hell is going on."

"Mona, did you just drop by to say hello or was there something you wanted?" Hayley interjected, trying to regain control of the conversation.

"Of course there's a reason I'm here. I'm not like

Liddy. I don't just drop in unannounced. That's downright rude, if you ask me. You always call first."

But she hadn't called.

Hayley decided to let that one slide by.

"I'm sure you'll want to hear this one. Rhonda and I got together tonight for dinner. . . ."

"I'm sorry. Rhonda?" Aaron asked.

"Yeah. Rhonda Franklin. I'm sure you've heard of her," Mona said, annoyed she had to fill in the details for Aaron, who was unfamiliar with the backstory.

"The TV star Rhonda Franklin?"

"Yes! How many frigging Rhonda Franklins do you think there are, Aaron? Anyway, we were having cocktails in her hotel room—"

"In her hotel room?" Aaron asked, stupefied.

"Have you been treating a lot of sick parrots at your vet practice lately, Aaron? Because you're starting to sound like one."

"Forgive me. I'm just a little surprised you spent the evening in Rhonda Franklin's hotel room. Isn't she a . . . ?"

"Lesbian. The word's lesbian. And yes, she is. We decided to dine in her room tonight since the paparazzi was camped outside the hotel and we didn't want to deal with all the cameras flashing and those nasty reporters screaming questions at her all night."

"It's just that you look so nice, like you were out on a date with your husband tonight."

"My husband hasn't left the house after the local news since 1998. I don't see what the big deal is. Liddy's always squawking at me to dress better. I just thought I'd make an effort, that's all. And can't a straight woman and a lesbian be friends without them being secret lovers? Rhonda and I are *friends*, okay? Is that against the law now?"

"I totally get it. My apologies. I won't say another word," Aaron said.

"Mona, I think it's wonderful that you've made a new friend, but I'm just concerned about Rhonda," Hayley said gently.

"Why?"

"Well, have you made it clear that your friendship is strictly platonic?"

"No, not in so many words. But she knows I'm not gay."

"Are you sure?"

"Of course I'm sure," Mona screamed before stopping herself and thinking about it. "I mean, pretty sure."

Hayley folded her arms and stared at Mona.

"Okay, I haven't exactly been up front about not being attracted to her in that way, but I'm having so much fun. She's a real hoot to hang out with, and I'm afraid if she finds out we'll never wind up in the sack together, she'll stop seeing me, and that would really bum me out."

"You *have* to tell her, Mona," Hayley said.

"I know. I know. Tonight after we chowed down on room service and were having a nightcap, she put a hand on my knee as she was making a point and left it there, and I was about to say something, but the yelling in the next room started and I got distracted."

"Who was yelling?"

"That's why I came over here. I knew you'd want to know. I know you're supposed to be the detective around here, Hayley, but you've got to step up your game. I'm the one who has been coming up with all the clues lately. First I see that two-bit floozy sneaking around with the German, and now I overhear a shouting match between her and her hippie boyfriend."

"Red? They're staying in the room next door?"

"Yeah. Rhonda told me they moved into the hotel to get away from Olivia's husband, Nacho, until the estate is settled and they get the house and can kick him out."

"Did Red find out she was cheating with Thorsten Brandt?"

"Oh yeah. There was a lot of banging and screaming, and I heard him tell her to get the hell out. They were done, over, kaput! She said she wasn't going anywhere and he threatened to call the cops. When she wouldn't budge, he actually did, and a few minutes later we heard Officer Donnie at the door and there was more yelling and crying. And Officer Donnie said the room was registered to Red so if he wanted her to go she had to go, and she still refused, so he had to escort her out by force. We heard her screaming all the way down the hall until he got her on the elevator and the door closed. And then it got real quiet and the hippie didn't make another sound until I left."

"Thorsten clearly had an agenda. He wanted Olivia out of the way to clear the path for his expansion plans with the company. He could have been in cahoots with Peggy, who had an influence over Red," Hayley said.

"Listen, Hayley. I know we were going to have a talk tonight, but I have an early appointment tomorrow and really should go home and get some sleep."

"No, Aaron, I can call Mona later. . . ."

"It's all good. You stay, Mona. I'll call you tomorrow, Hayley."

Before Hayley could say another word, Aaron's jacket was in his hand and he was heading out the door past Mona.

"By the way, you look real nice tonight, Mona," he said, and then he was gone.

"He never said anything about how I look and he was here for two hours," Hayley said, shaking her head, not sure what to make of his strange behavior.

"Damn, Hayley. I busted up your date. I'm real sorry."

"It's fine, Mona. I get the feeling he didn't want to have any kind of serious discussion about our relationship."

"You still think he's going to propose?"

"I don't know. If he was, he obviously chickened out. Or he's having serious second thoughts."

Chapter 25

Hayley knew Sergio couldn't resist her bacon potato soup. She had also thrown in some crusty bread to dip in it and then drove straight over to the police station.

Sergio wasn't surprised to see her walk through the door bearing comfort food. In fact, he looked as if he had been expecting her.

It was a quiet Sunday night. The station was empty except for Officer Earl, one of Sergio's junior patrolmen, who sat behind his desk pretending to be filing a report, but Hayley could tell he was playing a video game on his computer. Her son, Dustin, had that same focused expression, quick flashes reflecting off his reading glasses, whenever he was wrapped up in *Arkham Knight*, zipping around in the Batmobile and taking down the bad guys.

Sergio waved Hayley into his office and she gave him a quick hug before making a beeline for his desk and unpacking the goodies she had brought.

"Randy said you were working late tonight, so I didn't want you to go hungry," Hayley said, pulling the lid off her Tupperware container and spooning the soup into a ceramic bowl.

The mouthwatering aroma wafted over to Sergio, who couldn't resist. He sat behind his desk, anxiously waiting to be served.

"Well, wasn't that nice of him. Did he tell you anything else?" Sergio said, eyeing her suspiciously.

"No," Hayley said innocently, presenting Sergio with her homemade soup.

He scooped up a spoonful and ate it.

His eyes closed.

He was obviously in a state of euphoria.

He savored the taste for a few more seconds before putting his spoon down. "You mean he didn't tell you I arrested Thorsten Brandt tonight?"

"Oh, that. He may have mentioned it. I plumb forgot."

"I bet you did. You couldn't get over here fast enough, could you?"

"I'll admit I have a passing interest in Mr. Brandt given his connection to Olivia Redmond and the trouble he was having with her and my run-in with him at the Wildwood Stables. But I came here because I love you, Sergio, and I know you work hard, and I just want to make sure you're eating properly. Now, is that a crime?"

"All right. We will pretend that's why you are here and I will tell you why I arrested Mr. Brandt."

"I assume you found some evidence linking him to Olivia Redmond's murder," Hayley said, inching closer, curious to know the truth.

"I have come across some evidence. But it does not connect him to Ms. Redmond's murder."

"Then what did he do?"

"I have cement proof—"

"Concrete."

"What?"

"It's 'concrete proof.' Not 'cement proof.'"

"Are they not the same thing?"

"Well, yes. But the saying is 'concrete proof.'"

"Why can't you Americans make anything easy? Fine! Concrete proof. I have concrete proof that he put that burr underneath the saddle of the horse that threw you and nearly broke your spine yesterday."

"What? Did a witness come forward?"

"Better than that. I have digital photos."

Sergio turned his computer screen around and opened a file. Five rows of very crisp, clear photographs popped up, all of the family of tourists whom Hayley ran into at the Wildwood Stables.

The mother and her two kids.

The dad was obviously the one who took the photos.

In the background of roughly half of them, Hayley could make out Thorsten Brandt approaching Lightning, then clearly wedging the burr beneath the horse's saddle and then casually handing him off to the stable boy, who brought him over to Hayley to ride.

"Oh my God," Hayley said.

"The daughter uploaded the photos on her iPad when the family returned to the campground where they're staying. She noticed right away, so they called me and came over to show me. I immediately got a warrant and sent Donnie and Earl to pick him up."

"What did you book him on?"

"Attempted murder. And that's not all. This afternoon a Redmond employee, a whistle-blower, e-mailed a number of documents to the feds. All were very specific examples of Brandt's rampant corruption and questionable business dealings. He was operating a massive embezzlement scheme. He was taking out loans on behalf of Redmond Meats for his expansion plans and transferring the bulk of the money to dummy accounts overseas. He knew once the company's financial officers realized something was wrong, he would be long gone and the company would be forced to file for bankruptcy."

"Did Olivia discover what he was doing? Is that why he killed her?"

"I don't know if he killed her. I have no evidence that incriminates him other than he didn't like her and she was refusing to bend to his will. The feds are convinced he's our killer. I am basically holding him until they get here and can question him. I tried getting him to talk to me, but he kept his mouth shut. I don't see him talking to the government guys either. He's already put in a call to a very high-powered lawyer."

"Can I get some face time with him?"

"You know I can't do that, Hayley. Besides, why would he talk to you? He tried to bump you off on the carriage trails."

Hayley held up the Tupperware container that had a healthy serving of bacon potato soup left in it. "Maybe he's hungry."

"You know I am the chief of police and cannot allow a civilian to communicate with a murder suspect."

"I would never want to get you in any kind of trouble, Sergio. I understand."

"Although I will tell you I am thirsty and could

use a soda. The machine is down the hall. I could be gone for five, maybe ten minutes. No more than ten minutes. And then I will be back here in my office expecting to see you just where I left you."

Sergio stared at Hayley.

She knew the drill.

He was not willing to give Hayley permission to talk to Brandt in his cell. But he would not be at fault if she took matters in her own hands and did it on her own when he wasn't around. That would absolve him of all responsibility.

"Do you need change for the machine?"

Sergio shoved a hand in his pants pocket and jangled some coins. "I'm all set. I guess I will head to the soda machine now."

He whistled a tune as he strolled out of the office.

Hayley waited a few seconds and then poked her head out the office door.

The coast was clear.

She dashed down the hall with her Tupperware container to the row of cells in the back of the station.

She found Thorsten Brandt, his shirt open, an untucked T-shirt underneath. A hangdog expression on his face.

He was not happy to be here and he was depressed that his life as he knew it was basically over.

When he saw Hayley, he frowned. "I did not expect to see you here," he said. "What do you want?"

She handed him the Tupperware container and a plastic spoon through the bars of the cell. "It's my bacon potato soup. Very hardy. Much tastier than the slop they serve here. Enjoy."

"Is this some kind of incentive for me to bare my soul to you?"

"No. But it is so delicious there's no telling what you might admit."

"The chief showed me the photos. I know I'm caught red-handed. I never meant to hurt you. I only wanted to scare you. I did not want you exposing my . . . never mind."

Thorsten took a mouthful of soup and closed his eyes.

He dropped the spoon and began slurping the soup down directly from the Tupperware container until it was all gone.

"I take it you like my soup," Hayley said.

He shrugged. "It's okay. Could use a little more salt."

He loved it. He just wasn't about to admit it.

"Did you kill Olivia Redmond, Thorsten?"

He threw the Tupperware to the floor. "No, I did not! And if you say that again, I'll sue for defamation."

"You're in jail for attempted murder and embezzlement. There's not much left of you to defame."

"I had nothing to do with Olivia's murder. In fact, I have an airtight alibi. I was whale watching with my secretary, who accompanied me here. I'm sure the crew as well as a few other tourists on the boat remember seeing us. We are probably in some of their pictures. Now, that's all you get. I'm not talking anymore without my lawyer present."

"Why did you tell me anything? Do you like my soup that much?"

"No. I feel bad about what happened at the stables. I was not thinking clearly. I should not have pulled that stunt. But I panicked. We are done here. Now go, please."

Hayley nodded and raced back down the hall.

She knew her ten minutes were just about up and she had to get back to Sergio's office before he returned with his can of Dr. Pepper.

Despite him nearly paralyzing her in the park, she suspected Thorsten was telling the truth.

He did not kill Olivia.

She was more useful to him alive. He needed her to still be the face of the company until he was finished bleeding it dry and absconding with millions in company funds.

Someone snapping Olivia's neck in the garden was not a part of his plan.

Island Food & Spirits
by
Hayley Powell

The other night after getting off the phone with my mother from our biweekly phone call, I got an incredible urge for a Bacon-Wrapped Pork Tenderloin. Craving meat after speaking with my mother is a Pavlovian response from childhood. When my brother and I were kids, our mother's idea of meat was a veggie dog or tofu brushed in BBQ sauce and browned on the grill. And everyone knows when you deprive a child of any food their friends are allowed to eat on a regular basis, they just want it more!

When I was around twelve years old I was suddenly introduced to the wonderful world of pork.

My mother worked one week a month at the local retirement community village where she was in charge of collecting the residents' monthly rent.

This was a job she absolutely loved and took very seriously. She was very proud of her 100 percent rent collection record each month.

She would actually prepare a plan of attack and approached her task with a military-like precision and an enthusiasm that I didn't quite understand at such a young age. She seemed to enjoy taking me along with her. It was only later that I realized she had ulterior motives.

Sometimes she would sit me down in the common room. The nice elderly people were so happy to see a lively young child because I reminded them of their own grandchildren. They would always come up and speak to me. Then my mother would suddenly appear out of nowhere right in front of the poor old soul, startling them, with her hand out, unblinking, and request their monthly rent check. Her intended target would begin stammering an excuse about how she had left her wallet in her apartment. That didn't deter my mother. She just placed an arm around her prey and headed her in the direction of her apartment, stuck to her side the whole way.

On a few occasions she would even have me wear my Girl Scout uniform and place me in front of an unsuspecting resident's door as if I was selling cookies, and then she would rap sharply on the door and hang back by the wall. Once the poor senior looked out of his peephole and just saw an adorable young girl in her scout uniform presumably selling cookies, he would then walk right into my mother's ingenious trap. He would open the door and my mother would pounce, like a cat on a mouse. She would casually slip her foot in far enough so the door couldn't be closed and, with a bright smile on her face, say something like, "Mr. Foster, I'm so glad I caught you at home. Would you like to pay your rent?"

What does all this have to do with pork? Well, even though I felt bad being a pawn in my mother's scheme to hold on to her perfect rent collection record, I did find a beacon of shining light at this facility, and it was in the form of the residents' dining hall.

One day after helping my mother catch yet another victim, she sent me off to the residents' dining hall to get a bite to eat, and let me tell you, I never looked back.

It was a beautiful place filled with every imaginable delectable meat dish my young mind could conjure up, and I set out to try every last one of them while my mother was busy working her stealth maneuvers to track down every last senior who owed her money.

It was heaven!

One dish I couldn't get enough of was the Bacon-Wrapped Pork Tenderloin. It was divine! And in my young mind, this mouthwatering treat ran circles around my mother's bland, chewy tofu dogs.

But, as they say, all good things must come to an end, and for my mother and me they did rather quickly after one particular incident that may have been over the top even for my mother.

One day at work with my mother, I was just leaving the dining room after gorging on yet another meal of Bacon-Wrapped Pork Tenderloin when I heard yelling coming from the residents' common room. I dashed off to see what was going on, arriving in time to see an unconscious woman being wheeled away on a gurney by the EMTs after suffering some kind of malady. My mother, who had apparently jumped up on the gurney and was practically on top of the poor woman, reached into her purse, all the while yelling to all of the stunned residents and staff who were frozen in place, that she knew poor Mrs. Clark would be horrified if her rent had been late while she was in the hospital, and how she wanted to relieve her mind knowing her bills had been paid on time.

That was the end of my mother's job as the rent collector at the senior retirement village. It also meant the end of my meat-eating days in the dining hall. But it was too late to go back to fake meat. I was a goner. And after teaming up with my brother, we staged a revolt. My mother finally gave in and we were officially a family of carnivores.

But that is another story.

So in salute of my happy meat-eating youthful memories, I'm sharing one of my favorite recipes, Easy Bacon-Wrapped Pork Tenderloin. I'm also including my mother's favorite cocktail—a Gin Fizz that she always drank as a reward for a job well done after collecting all those rent checks.

Gin Fizz

<u>Ingredients</u>

3 ounces of your favorite gin
1 tablespoon superfine sugar
3 tablespoons fresh lemon juice
Ice
Seltzer

Add the first four ingredients to a shaker and mix together, then pour into a tall glass. Top with seltzer water and cheers!

Easy Bacon-Wrapped Pork Tenderloin

<u>Ingredients</u>
1 pork tenderloin, 1½ pound
3 tablespoons brown sugar
2 teaspoons kosher salt
1 teaspoon smoked paprika
Pinch of cayenne (more or less to
 your taste)
6 slices your favorite bacon (or
 enough to completely wrap)
1 tablespoon vegetable oil
¼ cup mango chutney (or your favorite flavor)
2 tablespoons whole grain mustard

Preheat your oven to 350 degrees.

Open the pork loin and make sure you pat it dry; set aside on a cutting board or platter.

Combine the brown sugar, salt, paprika, cayenne in small bowl, then rub the mixture all over the pork tenderloin.

Wrap the bacon around the tenderloin, securing with toothpicks.

Heat vegetable oil over medium-high heat until hot in a large cast iron pan and place the bacon-wrapped tenderloin in the pan and sear. Do not try turning to the other side until bacon is nice and dark brown. Cook each side for at least 6 to 8 minutes.

Mix the chutney and mustard in a small bowl and when bacon is done, generously brush the mixture on the top and sides of the tenderloin in the skillet, then transfer the skillet to the oven for about 15 minutes or when a thermometer reads 140 F. Remove from oven, tent with foil, and let rest for 10 to 15 minutes.

Remove the toothpicks, slice, and eat up!

Note: We like using the leftover chutney in the jar as a dipping sauce.

Chapter 26

"I have it right here on my computer screen, Hayley," Candy Pryor said on the other end of the phone. "The photo was taken on the seventeenth. Same day as when poor Mrs. Redmond was murdered."

Candy worked for her family's whale-watching expedition company, which departed three times a week from the town pier.

"We put out a giant cardboard cutout of a whale on the dock about an hour before we set sail, and everybody who buys a ticket stops and has their picture taken with it, and then we print them out and sell them in the gift shop to anyone who wants them after the boat gets back. It was my dad's idea after seeing it done at Disney World when he took the grandkids last winter."

"And you're sure it's Thorsten and his secretary?"

"Hold on. I'll e-mail it to you."

After a few seconds there was a ding alerting Hayley to an incoming e-mail. She opened the file attached, and sure enough, there was Thorsten in cargo shorts and a polo shirt with a light sweater tied around his neck, and his secretary, a young woman no more than thirty with a fresh-faced smile, her auburn hair blowing in the breeze, who wore a tight-fitting pair of jeans, a pink blouse, and a bomber jacket. They were holding hands and smiling.

They looked like a couple on a romantic outing.

Except for the fact that Hayley now knew Thorsten was also seeing Red's girlfriend, Peggy, on the side.

In addition to being an ethically challenged businessman, Thorsten Brandt was also a blatant womanizer.

"Looks like his alibi checks out," Hayley said.

"I remember him buying the tickets. He was very charming with that German accent, and he spent the whole time flirting with me while I ran his credit card through the machine. He's a very handsome man, don't you agree?" Candy said, giggling.

"Not my type. Thanks, Candy," Hayley said.

"Anytime, love. And be sure to come join us one of these days on an expedition if you don't get seasick. We'd love to have you."

"Yes, I'd love that," Hayley said, hanging up.

She had no real intention of taking Candy up on her kind offer. She had been wrestling with a fear of water ever since a cold-blooded killer had discovered she had connected him to his uncle's murder and taken her out to sea on a boat to dump her over the side so she couldn't tell anyone. Luckily the coast guard had shown up in the nick of time. Mona had begged her to try and get over her irrational fear by joining her on her fishing boat to haul lobster traps outside the harbor, but Hayley was still resistant. Liddy had tried talking her into planning a luxury cruise through the Caribbean on a boat so big she wouldn't even feel it moving. But so far Hayley was content to simply avoid sea travel altogether.

One of these days she would try to work through it.

Just not now.

Bruce bounded out to the front office from the bull pen. "Did Brandt's alibi check out?"

Hayley nodded. "Yes. He's officially off the suspect list."

"So are Red and Peggy. I was able to confirm they weren't even in town on the day of the murder. They traveled together by the company's private plane from California the day *after* Olivia's body was found. Red probably wouldn't even have bothered to come to Bar Harbor because of his fractured relationship with his mother, but he saw a big payday with his mother's will."

"I'm sure Peggy did too," Hayley added. "As well as the opportunity to spend some time with her secret lover, Thorsten. I checked the social registers for several Redmond Meats parties in New York and both Peggy and Thorsten's names were on the guest list for one at the Met and one at Lincoln Center. I'm sure that's where they met. Even though Red despised his mother and most likely didn't want to attend, I'm sure Peggy pressured him into going since she loves high society and is so desperate to be a part of it."

"Good work. See? Working together is fun," Bruce said, grinning.

"We are *not* working together. We just work in the same office and just happen to be investigating the same case and are simply choosing to share information."

"However you want to see it," Bruce said, pouring himself a cup of coffee. "Of course, if you *were* my partner and not my competitor, I would tell you what I was able to find out about Rhonda Franklin."

Checkmate.

He had her.

Hayley stood up from her desk. "What did you find out, *partner*?"

Bruce chuckled. "You're so easy. I knew you'd see the light."

"Tell me, Bruce."

She was wild with curiosity. She'd do anything to find out.

Within reason, of course.

"I did a little online digging this morning by Googling Rhonda Franklin and I found this brief story on a Web site called Deadline Hollywood about Rhonda being offered a role in a major motion picture about six months ago. Her agent was in negotiations with the studio, and she was requesting a leave from *The Chat* so she could go shoot the movie in Texas. But then, just two days later, there was a follow-up piece announcing that Rhonda had pulled out of the picture and was going to be replaced by another actress."

"So? Actors leave projects all the time because of scheduling conflicts, or personal reasons, or just about anything."

"Yeah. I get that. But I went through Rhonda's tweets during that time, and she was clearly excited about doing the movie and couldn't stop talking about what a juicy role it was, and how grateful she was to be given such a fantastic opportunity to do a film of substance. I mean, she didn't hold back. This was *huge* for her."

"Then why would she drop out?"

"Exactly. I called her agent and manager and they never got back to me. I tried getting hold of anyone who worked on *The Chat* who might have an inkling about what happened and got nothing. But then I did a search on *When the Cows Come Home* and that's when I hit pay dirt."

"*When the Cows Come Home*?"

"Yeah, that's the movie's working title. The story is all about the evils of the meatpacking industry. It's a downright exposé. Remember when Oprah Winfrey lambasted the beef industry on her show and they sued her? Imagine how they would feel if a national spokesman for one of the leading meat companies in the world was to play a major part in a movie that basically indicted their business practices?"

"That would not be kosher, so to speak," Hayley said.

"I called the producers and once again they refused to talk to me. But then I e-mailed the director, who is this wunderkind talent, very young and brash and not afraid of controversy, and he called me right away after I sent him my phone number. He told me he wanted to cast Rhonda *because* of her connection to Redmond Meats. He wanted to stir things up. Make a statement. The studio backed him one hundred percent, and Rhonda was thrilled to be given such a meaty part—pardon the pun."

"I can't pardon that, Bruce. I just can't."

Bruce smiled. "He told me Redmond Meats

threatened to sue Rhonda for breach of contract if she did the film. Lawyers were brought in. It became a real standoff. But then Rhonda blinked first. She pulled out. The part was rewritten and they cast Naomi Watts and they wrapped shooting about a month ago. And now there is all this Oscar buzz for Watts. The director told me Rhonda was just devastated. She's never gotten over it, and now that there's all this adoring press for Watts even before the film's release, it's got to be killing her all over again. The director heard through mutual friends that Rhonda blames Olivia personally for sabotaging her chance for a real acting comeback, especially now with all the Oscar talk. She's still mad as hell, probably even more so now."

"Mad enough to kill Olivia?"

Chapter 27

A loud crash startled Rhonda Franklin, and she jumped and spilled white wine all down the front of her blouse. "What the hell was that?"

Hayley bolted from the couch and ran into the kitchen where she found Pork Chop sitting innocently next to the coatrack, which he had somehow knocked to the floor. Blueberry was backed into a corner, hissing and baring his teeth, while Leroy ran behind Hayley's leg, shaking, scared he might be blamed for Pork Chop's antics.

"How did you get out of the basement?" Hayley asked, spinning around to see the door leading down into the cellar wide open, the flimsy latch that hooked into the lock lying on the rug. "Did you bust the lock? Bad pig! Bad pig!"

"Is that my baby?" Rhonda cooed as she hustled into the kitchen and squatted down to pet the snorting animal. "I just love this pig. He's the most darling thing I've ever seen. I didn't know you were still looking after him."

"It seems Red doesn't want anything to do with

him," Hayley said, taking Rhonda's wineglass and refilling it with some more Chardonnay. "I'm sorry Mona didn't make it tonight. One of her kids has the sniffles and it's her husband's poker night, so she's stuck at home."

"Well, I'd be lying if I told you Mona wasn't a big reason I accepted your kind invitation for cocktails this evening. She's so warm and kind and thoughtful."

"Are you sure we're talking about the same Mona? Mona Barnes?"

"Yes. I've never met anyone quite like her, and let me tell you, I've been around."

"Well, Mona likes you too. Sorry. I know I'm a poor substitute."

"Don't be silly. I'm having fun. And now that my little rascally, adorable pig is here, the night just got even better!"

Unable to squat anymore, the rotund Rhonda Franklin scooped the pig up in her arms and let him nestle against her bosom as she tried climbing back up to her feet, using her hip against the dishwasher to give herself an extra heave-ho.

Pork Chop closed his eyes, his expression euphoric as Rhonda lowered her face and nuzzled his snout with her nose.

"How could Red not want to cuddle with you all night? Because he's a stupid dolt, that's why, and he doesn't deserve you. No, he doesn't. You are a VIP! A very important pig!"

Boy, Rhonda sure did love this pig.

It was honestly a tad disconcerting.

Blueberry, tail high in the air, marched out of the room in a snit, obviously jealous he was garnering zero attention from Hayley's guest. Leroy remained hidden behind Hayley's leg until she moved to make herself another cocktail, and then he followed closely behind on her heel.

Rhonda downed her wine and casually held out her glass, indicating she was ready for yet another. Pork Chop settled into the crook of her arm and snorted contentedly as Rhonda scratched his belly while Hayley emptied the rest of the Chardonnay into her glass and tossed the empty bottle into her recycle bin.

"He really mellows out when he's around you, Rhonda. You should see him when you're not here. He's like a tornado!"

"We just have a special bond. Ever since Olivia first got him. She saw how I instantly fell in love with him at a barbecue on Olivia's estate in the Hamptons last summer, and she offered to find me a potbellied pig just like him, but I didn't want just any pig. This pig is the one who stole my heart," she said, kissing him on top of his head between his ears and then gratefully accepting more wine from Hayley.

After another sip, Rhonda cleared her throat. "So why did you really invite me here tonight, Hayley?"

"What do you mean?"

"I got the feeling when I arrived there was something you wanted to talk to me about. You kept waiting for the right moment to bring it up, but so far there hasn't been one. I don't like playing games, so why don't you just get to it?"

"Rhonda, I really thought Mona was going to come here tonight, and I know how fond of her you are, so this wasn't some ruse. . . ."

"Hayley, I was raised on Long Island and I know

when someone's feeding me a line of bull, so if you have something to say, just say it."

"I heard you and Olivia were not on the best of terms when she was murdered and I want to know——?"

"You want to know about the movie I was offered," Rhonda said.

"Yes. I know it caused a rift between the two of you."

"And so you want to know if I killed her?"

"If we're getting right to the point, then yes."

Rhonda set Pork Chop down on the floor, but he didn't take off to wreak more havoc. He stayed right by her side. Leroy glared at him from behind Hayley's leg but kept his faint growling in check.

"I admit I fantasized about killing her. When she forced me to drop out of that movie that would have changed my career, my whole life even, yes, I was bitter and angry. And there were days when my mind went to very dark places, and I wished she wasn't around to stop me from playing a once in a lifetime role. But they were just thoughts, Hayley. I would never seriously act upon them."

Hayley nodded, trying to read Rhonda's face, unable to tell if she was lying.

"I'm sure you read some of the filth in the supermarket tabloids. Saying how I'm twice Olivia's size, how I could have easily overpowered her and snapped her neck with my chubby hands. Those rags have always hated me, ever since I came out as a lesbian. They've been desperate to dig up dirt on me and sometimes they're right. I drink too much, I'm loud and obnoxious and can be a real ballbuster on the set of *The Chat*. But that's the extent of my obvious faults. I'm not a murderer. And the reason those stories faded is because the mainstream press actually bothered to check out my alibi. I wasn't even here when Olivia was murdered. I was in Delaware on the doorstep of a seventy-five-year-old fan, a grandmother, who won our Queen for the Day sweepstakes. I was personally delivering her a check for twenty grand and two free tickets for a seniors cruise to Alaska. I had a camera crew with me willing to testify I was there. I was out having fajitas at an Applebee's near Wilmington when I got word that Olivia was dead. . . ."

Her voice trailed off. Her eyes filled with tears.

"I miss her, Hayley. I really do. Despite what went down between us, she was my best friend."

Rhonda Franklin was an actress.

Capable of putting on a powerhouse performance.

But Hayley's gut told her this wasn't a Rhonda Franklin acting exercise.

She was hurting.

Deeply.

And Hayley at that moment knew Rhonda had nothing to do with what had happened to Olivia Redmond.

The killer was still out there.

Chapter 28

Hayley couldn't recall Bruce Linney ever begging for anything. He prided himself on being a cool, unflappable reporter. Emotional outbursts were not a part of his DNA.

And yet, here he was in the office of the *Island Times*, on his knees, his hands clasped in front of his face, pleading with Hayley.

Hayley couldn't deny she was enjoying being in the power position.

Just a little bit.

And Bruce knew it.

But that didn't stop him from this valiant effort to enlist Hayley's help in following a lead for his story on the murder of Dr. Alvin Foley.

"Hayley, please, I need you. She likes you."

"I'm sorry, Bruce. I want to go with you, but I'm way behind on my column, and Sal will kill me if I miss my deadline . . . again."

"It'll just take twenty minutes. I promise. I called Sherman's Bookstore and she's working there right now."

He wanted to question Carla McFarland.

But Carla despised Bruce.

He'd made the fatal mistake of remarking that Carla's double fudge brownies tasted like they came out of a box instead of made from scratch when he was judging a baking contest at the Blue Hill Fair three years ago.

Bruce had been dead to her ever since.

And there was no way she would actually talk to him if he showed up at the local bookshop where she worked part-time to ask her a few questions.

Which was why he needed Hayley.

He was able to confirm through conversations with a couple of Dr. Foley's colleagues at the Jackson Lab that he had been casually dating a local woman.

And after some more digging, Bruce had finally come up with a name.

Carla McFarland.

His heart sank.

He knew how Carla felt about him.

She'd told him so to his face when they ran into each other at a dinner party shortly after the Blue Hill Fair incident. Carla had let loose with a litany of expletives, causing so much tension Bruce had to excuse himself and leave before dessert was served.

A halfhearted apology e-mail did little to repair the damage. So Bruce just wrote her off. When was he ever going to have use for Carla McFarland anyway?

Famous last words.

But as luck would have it, Carla and Hayley were friends. Their sons, Dustin and Spanky, had been close pals and hung out after school all the time. The two mothers had also cochaired a PTA committee and chaperoned a junior high school dance when their sons were in the eighth grade.

Of course Carla would be open to talking to Hayley. Just not Bruce.

"I'll buy you lunch afterward. Anywhere you want. You like the mac and cheese at the Side Street Café. We can go there."

It was tempting. Bruce was pulling out all the stops.

Hayley was obsessed with the mac and cheese at the Side Street Café.

"I'll even order us the spinach artichoke dip!"

It was sad that Hayley could be bribed with food. But she couldn't resist the spinach artichoke dip.

She grabbed her coat and followed him out the door to his car. Her column was just about finished anyway, and Sal was out of the office covering a local court case. There really was no reason why she couldn't slip out of the office for a little while.

She just loved seeing Bruce beg.

When Hayley and Bruce arrived at Sherman's Bookstore on Main Street, they found Carla stocking the mystery section.

"Hi, Hayley!" Carla said in a cheery voice as Hayley rounded the corner.

Her smile quickly faded as Bruce fell in behind her. "Hello, Bruce," Carla said, her voice suddenly grim.

Carla pulled three copies of the new Joanne Fluke mystery out of a box and added them to the shelf.

"I love that blouse you're wearing," Hayley said, buttering her up.

"You do? I got it on sale at JC Penny. I thought the

colors might be too bold to wear at work, but the girls here love it. I've been getting compliments all morning."

"It's really nice," Bruce said, jumping in with a smile that looked more like a dog baring its teeth at an intruder.

"Who asked you?" Carla said coldly.

"Don't mind Bruce. He just gave me a ride here. Carla, I came here because I just found out you had been personally involved with Dr. Foley. . . ."

"Yes. He loved my double fudge brownies," she said pointedly in Bruce's direction.

"Well, I am so sorry for your loss," Hayley said.

"I still don't believe it. I mean, I'm used to men leaving me. Spanky's deadbeat dad, that Irish bartender last summer . . . So when Alvin disappeared I just assumed he got a better job somewhere else and didn't have the guts to dump me properly. But then, when his body turned up in the park . . . It's just so awful."

Carla moved to hug Hayley, and as she did she knocked the box of books she was stacking off the wooden stool it was resting on, and it crashed to the floor.

Bruce knelt down to pick up the books. "Here. Let me help."

"I don't want your help," she said, her tongue dripping with venom.

"Let him, Carla. It'll keep him busy while we talk," Hayley said.

Carla nodded and they stepped over Bruce and walked to the back of the store to the children's books section where they had more privacy.

"Why would anyone want to kill Alvin? He didn't

have a mean bone in his body. He was so gentle and sweet, and I thought he might finally be the one. . . ." Carla said, her voice trailing off, her eyes watering.

"Was he stressed out at work? Was he working on some kind of big project that might have put him in danger?"

"Not that I know of. Just the usual research. He didn't talk about his job much. I think he liked to put it out of his mind when he wasn't working at the lab."

"Did you notice any strange behavior before he disappeared? Or see him with anyone you didn't recognize?"

"No. The week he disappeared everything seemed so normal. We chatted on the phone a couple of times. We talked about driving to Kennebunk and booking a bed and breakfast for a romantic weekend in June. Then a couple of nights before he vanished, we went out to dinner. But it was just all so ordinary. He gave no indication anything was wrong."

"When was the last time you saw him?"

"The day after we had dinner. I dropped off some of my homemade chicken soup."

"Is that something you did regularly?"

"No. He wasn't feeling well and my soup is very medicinal. It can cure anything!"

"What was wrong with him?"

"I'm not sure. He was convinced he got food poisoning at the restaurant the night before. Bad oysters, I think. He was so sick he was ready to call the Health Department and have the restaurant shut down, but I talked him out of it because we weren't one hundred percent sure it was the restaurant and the owner is a friend."

"Where did you dine that night?"

"The Blooming Rose."

Felicity Flynn-Chan's bistro.

Olivia Redmond had also dined there the night before she was murdered.

And in Hayley's mind, that was too much of a coincidence.

Chapter 29

*If your idea of a memorable culinary experience is to find yourself slumped over the toilet all night hurling your guts out and your whole body shaking uncontrollably, then by all means make a reservation at the Blooming Rose in Town Hill. After hearing great things about the menu from some colleagues at the Jackson Lab, I took my girlfriend for dinner there last night. I ordered the oyster appetizer and must have gotten a bad one, because by the time I got home I was already feeling nauseous. I hold owner Felicity Flynn-Chan personally responsible for not properly inspecting the food she serves. Diners beware! I'm giving this place zero out of five stars! —**Dr. Feel Bad***

It didn't take a crack detective to deduce the author of the review on TasteTest, a user friendly Web site where consumers could post write-ups about their various dining experiences. Dr. Feel Bad gave the Blooming Rose a zero-star rating, dragging down the bistro's overall average. The date the review was posted was two days after Carla had gone to dinner with Dr. Foley at the restaurant, when he'd been feeling slightly better but was still furious over being served bad oysters. Dr. Foley disappeared just two days after posting the review.

Hayley had rushed home to scroll the Blooming Rose reviews on the site after Carla had casually mentioned that Alvin considered himself a food connoisseur and often wrote reviews whenever they dined out. Most of his other reviews were positive and upbeat. This was the only scathing one.

Hayley scrolled down for more recent reviews. There was a long list of four- or five-star ratings.

If she had thought to write her own review after dining at Felicity's establishment, she certainly would have given the place five stars.

She came across one more bad review.

*There is something fishy going on at the Blooming Rose! Owner Felicity Chan-Flynn has skated by for years on her restaurant's sterling reputation, but it's high time someone expose this eatery for what it really is—an overrated tourist trap that serves day-old fish and warmed up slop more in keeping with the menu at the state penitentiary rather than a high quality summer season restaurant frequented by visiting celebrities and dignitaries. I have already contacted writers for the top food magazines in New York to let them know that the Rose isn't blooming at all. It's wilting and past its prime. —**Meat Maven**

Ouch.

Even worse than Dr. Foley's review.

And Meat Maven was the obvious user name for Olivia Redmond.

She had posted it the morning after Hayley dined with her and Nacho at Felicity's restaurant.

And she was dead just a few days later.

Hayley didn't know what to think.

Was Felicity unhinged and scarily sensitive?

A crazed killer hell-bent on taking out anyone who spoke ill of her restaurant?

But Felicity could not have been the one to murder Olivia Redmond.

She had an airtight alibi.

She had already left the estate and was working in her vegetable garden back at the restaurant when Olivia was killed at the estate. She even had an eye-witness to corroborate her story who was willing to testify to the fact.

There was a knock at the back door.

Hayley looked up from her laptop, startled. She set the computer down next to Leroy, who was snoozing on the couch next to her, and walked through the kitchen and opened the door to find Bruce standing there.

"Is this a bad time?"

"No, come in," Hayley said.

Bruce looked around the kitchen as he entered. "You in the middle of making dinner?"

"I haven't really been cooking much since the kids aren't around."

"Oh, I see." He looked disappointed.

"Why? Are you hungry?"

"A little. Just thought I'd guilt you into letting me stay for dinner if you had a meat loaf in the oven or something."

"Sorry. What is it you want, Bruce?"

He glanced at the fridge. "You really don't have something hidden away in there you could whip up for the two of us?"

"Are you serious? There's nothing in the fridge. And even if there was, I don't feel like cooking you dinner!"

"Okay, fine. I get it. I'm not the handsome vet you've got the hots for. I'm just your platonic coworker so I get no special treatment."

"The point, Bruce. Get to the point. Did you really just stop by to get a free meal?"

"No. I went and found a busboy who works at the Blooming Rose after our conversation with Carla McFarland. Or to be clear, *your* conversation. Kid by the name of Jay Chaplin. Parents are teachers at the school. I know the family. He's a good egg."

"What did he have to say?"

"Once I got him to open up, he actually had a lot to say. His parents forced him to quit about a month ago. According to him, Felicity Flynn-Chan was a monster to work for."

"That's no surprise. She's always been a perfectionist. I know that because she calls me when she wants to place an ad for her restaurant in the *Island Times* and she will only deal with me because she wants it done just so."

And two lousy reviews on a well-trafficked Web site would undoubtedly send her into an emotional tailspin.

"She screamed at the poor kid all the time for the

silliest offenses, like forgetting to put the soupspoon in the right space on the table or if on a busy night he didn't clear a table fast enough. The stress was so bad he went to the doctor and was given a prescription for an antidepressant."

"A lot of restaurant owners are mercurial and demanding, Bruce."

"Yeah, but this apparently went way beyond that. One night a table complained that the basket of bread they had been served wasn't warm enough and she had such a meltdown she spent the rest of the night curled up in a ball in a corner of the kitchen and wouldn't talk to anyone. Another time she beat one of her waiters with a spatula for dropping a pat of butter into the lap of a state senator who was dining with her husband. He had a zillion stories like this. God forbid you get on her bad side."

"So she's unstable. That doesn't make her a killer," Hayley said.

"Man, all this talk about food . . . I'm starving."

"Off topic, Bruce."

"Right. Maybe she's not a killer. But I not only talked to Jay, I got in touch with a dishwasher and a hostess and a couple of waiters, and they all said the same thing. Felicity Flynn-Chan is nuts and willing to do just about anything to protect her business. The only thing she loves more than that restaurant is her husband, Alan. She's completely devoted to him."

Alan Chan.

Felicity's subdued, nondescript husband.

The restaurant's well-trained chef who remained safely tucked away in his wife's shadow.

Felicity was the true face of the operation.

And she may have had an alibi for Olivia's murder.

But did Alan?

"Want to order a pizza with me? We can have it delivered. My treat," Bruce said, clutching his growling stomach.

It dawned on Hayley that she had no idea what she was going to have for dinner, so resigned, she shrugged. "Fine. Have a seat in the living room. I'll call Little A's and pop open a couple of beers."

Bruce beamed from ear to ear as he shook off his jacket and hung it on the coatrack, then pulled out his cell phone. "I'll call. Meat lover's okay?"

She nodded as she watched him laconically drift into the living room and turn on a cable news channel. Hayley had to give him credit. His persistence had paid off.

Bruce Linney was staying for dinner.

Island Food & Spirits
by
Hayley Powell

The other night I showed up at my brother Randy's, bar with my yummy Skillet Bacon Mac & Cheese because his husband, Sergio, was working late wrapping up a couple of big cases and I didn't want Randy skipping dinner. It was also an excuse to get one of Randy's signature Blackberry Moonshine Cocktails, which I was sure my grateful brother would offer on the house.

As we sat at the bar chowing down on the mac and cheese and sipping our cocktails, a childhood friend of ours, Jeff Pryor, sauntered into the bar to grab a beer, so we waved him over to join us since we hadn't seen him in a while. We all began to catch up on what was going on in each of our lives. Most of you probably know that Jeff owns a sightseeing cruise boat that takes visitors around Mount Desert Island and the outer islands where they can take in the rocky, beautiful coast as well as look at seabirds, seals, and some of the lavish summer homes of the rich and famous.

He also offered a sunset cocktail cruise that is a favorite among many folks, myself included.

I know, I know, you're not surprised.

As we were chatting away, a young off-duty summer park ranger strolled in and took a seat at the bar to enjoy a cold beer before heading home, presumably after a long day at work.

I noticed a young couple sitting next to us at the bar with a stack of brochures from the park headquarters in Hulls Cove. The woman got excited upon seeing the young park ranger and stood up and marched over to him, ignoring her husband's pleas to sit back down. She then tapped the ranger on the shoulder.

"Excuse me, may I ask you a question? My husband has been no help whatsoever," she said, tossing him a disgusted look over her shoulder.

"Of course," the ranger said, smiling. "What's your question?"

"At what age does a deer become a

moose? We haven't been able to find the answer in any of the brochures."

Randy spit out his Blackberry Moonshine Cocktail while Jeff and I both fought hard not to erupt in a fit of giggles.

The park ranger patiently explained that deer do not become moose. They stayed deer. The woman began arguing with the poor ranger and declared that he didn't know anything because she had seen a picture of a grown moose next to its baby deer with her own eyes. The ranger stood his ground. Moose are *not* grown-up deer. So with a huff, the woman spun around and grabbed her embarrassed husband and marched right out of the bar.

The second they were gone we all broke out into hysterical laughter.

When we finally calmed down, Jeff began to tell us some of the questions he gets on his various boat cruises.

"What do you do with the islands in the winter?"

We chuckled at this one.

"How many sunset sails do you do in a day?"

Now we were laughing.

"How long is your two-hour tour?"

Randy was practically choking after that one, and I was laughing so hard I could barely breathe.

"Is this island surrounded by water?"

Now we were rolling.

After just leaving the dock on the boat, one tourist actually looked back at where they had launched only moments before and asked, *"What town is that?"*

My sides hurt from laughing so hard.

But the one question that really got us going and caused me to fall on the floor laughing in hysterics was one Jeff got last summer. He would always take pictures of each couple or group on the boat, and told them that after the tour they could pick their pictures up in the gift shop at the dock if they would like theirs to keep.

This led one passenger to ask him with a straight face, *"How will we know which one is ours?"*

As anyone around here knows, summers can be very long and somewhat trying on the patience at times, especially in a busy tourist town such as ours.

So remember to try to take some time and relax, and just have some fun by getting together with friends for a fun dinner in or out. But certainly don't forget to add a great cocktail or two. You'll end up having a wonderful time and the summer won't be so stressful.

This week I'll get your party started
with my Skillet Bacon Mac & Cheese
recipe and Randy's Blackberry Moonshine Cocktail.

Skillet Bacon
Mac & Cheese

Ingredients

1 pound box shell macaroni (or your
    favorite)
1 teaspoon dry mustard
½ teaspoon cayenne pepper (or less if
    you don't like a touch of heat)
2 cups grated sharp cheddar cheese
1 cup grated Gruyère cheese
1 cup, plus ½ cup grated cheddar
    cheese
1¼ cups milk
1½ cups panko bread crumbs
2 tablespoons chopped fresh parsley
6 slices cooked crispy bacon; reserve
    ¼ bacon grease
Salt and pepper to taste

Roux Sauce Ingredients
¼ cup butter
¼ cup flour
3 cups milk

First make the Roux Sauce. In a
large cast iron skillet over medium-low
heat (any large oven-safe skillet), melt

the butter, whisk in the flour, stirring constantly until a paste is formed and bubbles a bit, about 2 minutes. Add the milk a little at a time, whisking constantly until the sauce thickens, and remove from heat.

Bring a pot of salted water to a boil and cook the pasta until almost al dente, but do not fully cook; drain and set aside.

Preheat your oven to 400 degrees. Put Roux Sauce back on low heat and stir in mustard and cayenne. Gradually add the cheeses while stirring constantly until all the cheese has melted. Add the additional milk, salt, and pepper to taste.

Add the cooked pasta and cooked crumbled bacon to the Roux Sauce in the large skillet.

In a bowl mix together the panko bread crumbs, chopped parsley, and reserved bacon grease, and top the mac and cheese, sprinkling evenly. If you desire, sprinkle a little more grated cheese on top of bread crumbs.

Bake 25 to 30 minutes or until top is browned and pasta is bubbly.

Blackberry Moonshine Cocktail

Ingredients
2 ounces blackberry-flavored moonshine
1 ounce fresh lemon juice
Splash of seltzer water
6 blueberries
2 strawberries
2 blackberries

In a shaker pour the moonshine,
lemon and add half the fruit and
muddle together. Strain into an ice-
filled cocktail glass and top with a
splash of seltzer and garnish with the
leftover fruit. This is definitely a great
way to start a party!

Chapter 30

"I don't know why you roped me into coming with you," Randy said as Hayley drove them in her car to Town Hill.

"Protection. You're my bodyguard. I don't feel safe going on my own," Hayley said, speeding up on the country road that led to the Blooming Rose bistro.

"What do you hope to possibly gain by poking a stick at Felicity? It's not as if she's going to tell you anything like, 'Oh, Hayley, I'm so happy you stopped by. I want to confess to shooting Dr. Foley and strangling Olivia Redmond. Shall I call the police or would you rather do it?'"

"She didn't strangle Olivia. I think she may have enlisted the aid of her husband."

"Alan? But he's so quiet and passive. He doesn't strike me as the type to commit murder."

"That's because we've rarely heard him speak. We don't really know what he's like, which is why I'm hoping he's there when we swing by the restaurant just to say hello and make a dinner reservation."

"She's going to be suspicious. They have these wild inventions now called computers and you can actually make reservations online."

"I'll just tell her we were passing by on our way home from Ellsworth and decided to pull in and make a reservation in person."

"I have this foreboding sense of danger, Hayley. My stomach is doing flip-flops. And since when do you consider me a bodyguard? My husband is the law enforcement official. I'm just a low-key nonviolent bar owner with incredible hair," Randy said, checking himself out in the side mirror.

"You know what they say. There is safety in numbers."

"Yeah, but if what you suspect is true, do we really stand a chance against a homicidal husband and wife hit team?"

Hayley didn't have an answer for that one. It was almost too preposterous to contemplate.

Felicity and Alan Chan cold-blooded killers?

Over a couple of lousy reviews on TasteTest?

Hayley pulled into the gravel parking lot. There was one car parked near the restaurant entrance—a black Volvo.

It was quiet. Just a light breeze and slight chill in the air. Rain was undoubtedly on the way. Typical late April Maine weather.

Hayley and Randy got out of the car and walked inside the restaurant.

It was very cold.

No heat.

And empty.

The upholstered chairs were upended on top of all the tables in the dining room, and the floor appeared freshly mopped. There was a scent of Pine-Sol or some other cleaning agent.

"Hello? Felicity? Alan? Hello?"

No response.

Hayley turned to Randy. "Let's take a look around."

"Have you forgotten about the car parked out front? Somebody is obviously here," Randy said, his voice cracking.

"There's no harm in making sure," Hayley said, heading off to the side office just past the hostess station.

"You know, just because you get off playing Miss Marple doesn't mean we're all good at breaking and entering and throwing ourselves headfirst into perilous situations," Randy said. "But I am hungry, so I'll go check out the kitchen."

Hayley poked her head into the office and glanced around.

It was immaculately kept.

Not a stray piece of paper out of place.

On the wall were various framed awards and endorsements from a number of media outlets. The restaurant was ranked third in a *New York Times* article entitled "The Best Seasonal Restaurants in Maine." Best crab cakes in a *Bon Appétit* list, "Seafood Favorites." A profile of Alan in the *Maine Food & Lifestyle* magazine.

Hayley browsed through the story, which detailed Alan's fairy-tale marriage to Felicity, his extensive culinary training in Europe, his upbringing in Seoul, South Korea. She stopped at one paragraph and read it over more carefully. The reporter had asked Alan about when he was a young man in his early twenties and in the military. Alan had proudly recounted his days as an officer in the ROK Special Forces and how he'd been trained in hand to hand combat and weapons for secret missions in North Korea. It had been an intense time in his life, and in the name of his country he did some things that were tough to forget.

The reporter then shifted the focus of the article back to Alan's love of food and his dream of one day owning his own restaurant, which had certainly come to pass.

ROK Special Forces.

South Korea's own version of the US Army Green Berets.

Brave operatives sent on covert missions to take out terrorists, rescue hostages, retrieve vital information.

Someone in ROK Special Forces would be totally capable of snapping a woman's neck.

Trained to do it, in fact.

Hayley removed the framed article from the wall and walked back through the dining room toward the kitchen where Randy was foraging for food.

"Randy, take a look at this. It's not exactly proof, but it certainly raises a lot of questions about Alan Chan. . . ."

She burst through the carved wooden swinging doors and stopped short.

Standing near the stove was Randy, his eyes wide with fear.

Alan Chan stood directly behind him, one hand

clamped firmly over Randy's mouth while the other held a steak knife to his throat.

"Alan, what are you doing? Let my brother go," Hayley pleaded, keeping her voice soft and trying to remain calm.

"Why did you come here? What do you know?" Alan spit out.

"We just stopped by to make a reservation, okay?" Hayley said, gently putting down the framed article on the kitchen counter and holding out her hands to show that she came in peace.

"You're lying. I heard you just now. You have something on me. . . ."

His eyes wandered to the framed article resting on the counter. "Why are you looking at that? What's in there that has you so curious?"

"Nothing. I'm just impressed with your history. You've accomplished a lot."

Alan's eyes darted back and forth.

He was panicky.

Nervous.

Randy struggled.

Alan gripped Randy's mouth tighter with his hand and pressed the knife deeper into his neck until a small trickle of blood dripped down his Adam's apple.

Hayley didn't want Alan losing it and slashing Randy's throat.

She had to keep him calm.

"Please, Alan, let Randy go. We're not here to cause you any trouble," she said, fighting to steady her voice.

There was a long, agonizing moment of silence as Alan's mind raced.

He flinched.

Unsure what to do.

His wife, Felicity, was not here to direct him, which was usually the case.

He slowly began to lower the steak knife.

When it was a safe distance from his jugular, Randy made a grab for it. He latched onto Alan's fist holding the knife and the two men fought for possession of it. They crashed against the stove top, and Hayley screamed, making a mad dash over to them to help her brother, who was losing. She whacked Alan on the wrist with her fist and his grip loosened and the knife fell to the floor.

Hayley scooped it up and held it out toward him. "Stop it, Alan! Stop it right now!"

Alan managed to shove Randy off him and grab him again from behind.

This time he had one arm wrapped around Randy's neck and a hand pressed against the side of his head. "Drop the knife or with just the right amount of pressure I will break his neck in less than a second!"

Hayley immediately dropped the steak knife.

It clattered to the floor.

Randy was gasping, having trouble breathing.

"Is that how you broke Olivia Redmond's neck?"

Alan's lip was quivering.

His ROK Special Forces training had kicked in, but emotionally, he was conflicted about what he was doing, and it showed on his face.

"Were you defending your wife, Felicity's, honor by killing both Dr. Foley and Olivia Redmond? Is that what happened, Alan? Were they trying to assassinate Felicity's reputation, knock a few stars off her stellar five-star rating, and so you took matters into your own hands?"

"You've got it half right," a voice said from behind her.

Hayley twisted around to find Felicity Flynn-Chan in a flowery print blouse and pink slacks and a yellow Crusher sun hat to keep her eyes shaded while she worked in the garden.

She clutched a gun that was pointed directly at Hayley.

"Alan only killed Olivia. I was the one who shot that sniveling science geek who dared dis my food!" she spit out.

Hayley sighed.

The rumors were true.

Felicity Flynn-Chan was a certifiable sociopath.

It was at that moment Hayley realized she should have listened to Randy.

They never should have come to the restaurant.

And both she and her brother were about to pay for that mistake with their lives.

Chapter 31

"Those two were ugly thorns in my beautiful rose garden. No one has *ever* criticized my restaurant! I've received the highest compliments from US senators and ex-presidents, movie actors and rock stars! Martha Stewart ate clams alfresco on my patio because all my tables inside were booked, and she loved it! Loved it! And then some nerdy nobody waltzes in here like he's a food critic for the *New York Times*, gorges on my oyster platter, and then has a little case of indigestion after he gets home to his sad little apartment and he dares blame *me*? And he even has the gall to write a scathing review for all to see? Do you think I'm going to let him get away with that?"

"It was a little more than indigestion, Felicity. It was food poisoning," Hayley said quietly, immediately regretting it.

Felicity waved the gun around angrily. "Who cares? He sullied my good name. And then, not even a month later, that snotty bacon bitch acts like the

Queen of England and dares to complain about my fish? Well, I was not going to stand for it! I had already rid the world of that useless Foley character. As much as I wanted Olivia Redmond wiped off the face of this earth, I was not going to tempt fate twice by killing again. No. That would be sloppy."

"So why not enlist the help of your beloved husband, your dear Alan, the love of your life, who would do anything for you?" Hayley said.

"Yes. It's not like he's never killed anyone. Hell, after his stint in Korea's Special Forces, it was second nature to him," Felicity said, shrugging. "It was even easier the second time around. Dr. Foley tried to run. I had to line up my shot in just a few seconds and get him before he disappeared behind the trees just the way my father taught me when he took me deer hunting when I was a little girl. Still, if I had missed and he had gotten away, it would have been very messy and complicated. But Olivia, she never saw it coming. Alan stalked her like a North Korean sentry and snuck up behind her, and with one quick snap of the neck, it was done. No fuss. No mess. He's not just an expert in the kitchen. He excels at killing too. Don't you, baby?"

Alan smiled at his wife.

A sick, demented, obsessive smile.

Mr. and Mrs. Whack Job.

Hayley made eye contact with Randy, who signaled her he was ready to make a move. Before she could even react, Randy nailed Alan in the foot with his shoe.

Alan howled in pain, loosening his grip slightly.

Randy seized the opportunity to raise his arm and drive his elbow into the bridge of Alan's nose.

Blood spurted everywhere as Alan let him go and grabbed for his face.

Felicity gasped and jerked the gun in Randy's direction.

Hayley knew she had to do something.

She lunged at Felicity and tried wrestling the gun away from her.

Felicity fought like a tigress, scratching and biting Hayley with all her might.

Hayley plucked the yellow sun hat off Felicity's head and jammed it over her face, blinding her and backing her up against the stove all the while still struggling for the gun.

Out of the corner of her eye, Hayley saw Randy jab a knee hard into Alan's solar plexus. He doubled over, briefly incapacitated.

But not for long.

Randy scooped up the knife from the floor and raced to help his sister, just as Felicity's finger twisted around the trigger of the gun and pulled back, firing off a shot in Randy's direction.

Randy stopped in his tracks, a pale, shocked look on his face.

For a brief moment, Hayley's heart sank.

Had her brother just been shot?

Randy felt his stomach, expecting blood to seep out of his shirt from the bullet wound.

But nothing happened.

Hayley quickly realized the bullet had knocked the knife right out of his hand and it was gone. She tightened her grip on Felicity's hand holding the gun and slammed it into the stove.

Once.

Twice.

Three times.

Until the gun went flying out of Felicity's hand.

It skidded across the floor and underneath the refrigerator.

Hayley shoved Felicity aside and ran to Randy, grabbed him by the shirtsleeve, and they raced out of the kitchen.

She glanced back in time to see Felicity snagging a broom and then crouching down to use the wooden handle to retrieve the gun from underneath the fridge. If she got hold of that gun, she would undoubtedly come after them to finish the job.

Hayley and Randy sprinted out the front door of the restaurant and headed toward her car in the gravel parking lot. But before they could reach it, Alan, a white towel pressed to his nose, burst out a back door, blocking their path. He stopped, glaring at them, bloodstains on the towel.

He was unarmed.

But he was also military trained.

And Randy's fighting skills, which he learned in a scene combat class while briefly attending the New York School of Dramatic Arts, may have helped him get the upper hand, along with the element of surprise.

But they were no match for Alan's training.

And Alan was now madder than a wet hornet and was not about to lose a fight twice.

Felicity came flying out the back door and joined

her husband, gun in hand, ready to finally settle the matter.

Hayley and Randy turned and hightailed it into the woods.

A couple of shots rang out, the bullets whizzing a safe distance past them, cracking a few branches on a couple of trees.

Unlike the mellower days of deer hunting with her father, Felicity was in a frenzied state and wasn't taking the precious time she needed to line up her shot in order to take down her prey.

Hayley and Randy ran deeper and deeper into the woods, whipping around to see Felicity in hot pursuit, her injured husband stumbling behind her.

They kept running.

Faster and faster, like they were competing in the Boston Marathon and were within spitting distance of the finish line.

But Hayley was a recreational runner. Two miles in the park was her limit.

Randy was a hiker, not a runner. His foot landed wrong on a rock and he twisted his ankle, falling to the ground.

Hayley snatched his shirt and hauled him to his feet, resting his arm around her neck and helping him as he jumped on one leg for cover behind a couple of birch trees in full spring foliage bloom.

They sunk to their knees and held each other.

"You keep going. I'll be fine," Randy said, gasping for breath.

"Forget it. I'm not leaving you."

Hayley poked her head around the tree to see if Felicity and Alan were in the vicinity, but she didn't see any sign of them.

"I think we lost them," she said.

They continued on slowly, Hayley's arm around her brother, as he hopped along as best he could, until they spotted a clearing. Beyond that was a thicket of trees through which they saw cars whizzing past.

It was the main road.

They exchanged relieved looks and managed to make it out of the woods to a ditch, climbing up on the side of the road.

They waited for a car to come along.

And one finally did.

A black automobile that was zipping along well above the speed limit.

Hayley waved it down as Randy sat down to massage his throbbing ankle.

The car slowed down.

The window on the passenger side lowered.

Felicity Flynn-Chan smiled menacingly at them.

"We've been out searching all over for you two—isn't that right, babe?"

She turned briefly back at her husband behind the wheel, who glowered at them, pieces of white tissue stuffed up his nostrils, sweat pouring down his face.

She raised the gun and rested it on the car door. "Get in. We're going to go on a nice little drive to a quiet place where we won't be disturbed."

There was no getting away now.

Suddenly a flashing blue light nearly blinded Hayley.

She covered her eyes to see a police cruiser approaching from the opposite direction.

Alan panicked and slammed his foot on the gas pedal.

The Volvo shot off straight at the police cruiser in

a high stakes game of chicken. The Volvo blinked first and swerved to the side, missing a head-on collision with the cruiser by mere inches. The car flew off the road and hit a tree with a sickening crunch.

Sergio and Officer Donnie jumped out of their squad car.

Officer Donnie ran to the Volvo while Sergio dashed over to Hayley and Randy.

Sergio's eyes widened with concern at the sight of his husband on the ground, clearly injured.

"It's nothing, Sergio, just a twisted ankle," Randy said, trying to be brave, but his voice was still shaky from their close brush with death.

"How did you know we were out here?" Hayley asked.

"We didn't. We got a call from a neighbor nearby who heard some shots and called nine-one-one. We were just on our way to check it out."

Hayley turned to see Officer Donnie handcuffing Felicity; her head was down and her hair was covering her face and her shoulders were hunched over like a woman defeated.

Her husband, Alan, was on the ground, scraped up pretty badly, his nose bleeding even worse now than back at the restaurant.

Their Bonnie and Clyde killing spree was mercifully over.

Chapter 32

When Sonny Lipton called Hayley at the *Island Times* and requested she come over to his law office immediately, she wasn't inclined to drop everything and rush right over. Sonny was a young up and coming lawyer and Liddy's current boyfriend, or gentleman friend, as she preferred calling him. He was also fifteen years younger than her, a sensitive topic Liddy did not relish discussing.

Hayley was slammed that morning. Not only was her regular column due for the paper, the acting CEO of Redmond Meats had e-mailed her asking if she would mind writing a tribute column remembering Olivia Redmond for the company Web site. She quickly agreed but was now swamped with deadlines.

She asked Sonny if she could stop by his office later, but he was insistent. Two minutes later she received an urgent text from Liddy ordering her to get her butt in the car and over to Sonny's office right now! She checked with Sal to make sure he didn't have a problem with her slipping out for a few minutes. He didn't. He never did. He never took his eyes off his desktop computer. He just waved her away and growled something about picking him up a Whoopie Pie from Epi Pizza on her way back.

Ten minutes later Hayley walked up the stairs of Sonny's office on the second floor of a white two-story building, the first floor housing the Swan Agency, which specialized in real estate sales and insurance.

Liddy greeted her in the small reception area. She was biting her lip and looked as if she was about to burst.

"Liddy, what is it? What's so important that it couldn't wait?"

Liddy bounced up and down on the soles of her feet. "Sonny swore me to secrecy, but you're my best friend—I tell you everything! That's what I told him! But he made me promise to keep my mouth shut until he had a chance to talk to you first!"

"Talk to me about what?"

Liddy bit her lip harder, trying to keep her mouth from opening and spilling everything. This looked like it was the hardest thing she'd ever had to do.

"Hayley, thanks for coming," Sonny said, his Brooks Brothers light blue shirt a tad wrinkled, his rolled up sleeves accentuating his muscled forearms, and his bright yellow tie with tiny sailboats loosened and askew.

He was a fine-looking young man.

Liddy had definitely scored.

"Come into my office so we can have a little chat," he said with a slight Maine accent he'd worked hard to get rid of at law school. "Liddy, do you mind waiting out here?"

"To hell with that! Hayley's my best friend! I'm

not leaving her side!" Liddy yelled, grabbing Hayley's hand and squeezing tightly. "She needs me for support."

"Is someone suing me?" Hayley asked, suddenly worried.

"No, nothing like that," Sonny said, ushering them into his office and closing the door. "Have a seat."

Sonny circled around his desk and sat down. He opened a file in front of him and pulled out a stack of papers.

Liddy plopped down in the only available seat in front of the desk.

Hayley felt like she was playing musical chairs.

And had lost.

Sonny looked up and glared at his girlfriend, who didn't notice Hayley standing awkwardly next to her. "Honey, do you mind?"

Liddy realized she was hogging the only chair and that this meeting had nothing to do with her, so she self-consciously stood up and offered Hayley the chair. "You better sit down for this."

Hayley gulped.

This did not sound good.

She did what she was told.

An agonizing few seconds passed by as Sonny flipped through the pages on his desk.

Liddy placed a comforting hand on Hayley's shoulders.

"As you may know, I've been doing some consulting work for the law firm in New York that represents Redmond Meats. . . ."

"I didn't know that. Congratulations," Hayley said, smiling.

"I did! He told me! But once again, all I hear from

him all day long is, 'Liddy, you can't go blabbing everything I tell you.'"

Sonny glared at Liddy, who motioned with her fingers that she was zipping her lips.

"Anyway, they've brought me in to assist the probate of Olivia Redmond's will. It's a very complicated document and I'm still sifting through all the articles, but one fact is perfectly clear. Olivia's husband, Nacho, and her son, Red, are going to get nothing."

"You mean they've been cut out?" Hayley gasped.

"Completely. A portion of her fortune will go to various charities that were dear to her during her life, and many of the properties and assets will be retained by the company, but a good chunk of the estate will go to the only one who truly loved Olivia unconditionally. . . ."

"Who?"

"Pork Chop," Sonny said with a straight face.

"The pig! Can you believe it?" Liddy screamed before catching herself and stepping back, clasping her hands and bowing her head, desperately trying to keep her mouth shut.

"There is a very clear and specific clause that states that Pork Chop is to enjoy the lifestyle to which he has become accustomed for the duration of his natural life, and that the animal's court-appointed guardian will retain control over all decisions and finances. After the pig's death, the remaining fortune will be left to the guardian to spend as he or she may see fit."

"Are you telling me that the potbellied pig tearing up my house as we speak is worth millions now?"

"Twenty million, to be precise," Sonny said, looking up from his papers.

"*Twenty* million?" Hayley gasped.

"After Red found out his mother was excising him entirely from the will, he filed a petition with the court to be named Pork Chop's guardian," Sonny said.

"Sneaky bastard!" Liddy hissed, unable to contain herself.

"But given the explicit and legally binding wishes of the deceased, the court is refusing to recognize him," Sonny said.

"Well, who *are* they recognizing?"

"You."

Hayley sat back in the chair looking blankly at Sonny.

What he had just said did not register.

At first.

And then, after a few seconds, the word clicked in her mind.

You.

"Me?" Hayley squeaked.

Liddy couldn't rein it in anymore. She exploded with joy, grabbing Hayley by the shoulders and shaking her. "That pig can tear up your house all he wants! You can just buy a new one! A much bigger one! Maybe a waterfront mansion next to the Rockefellers!"

"Sonny, you can't be serious," Hayley said, shell shocked.

"If this plays out as I expect it will, you're going to come out of this a multimillionaire."

Hayley gripped the sides of the chair, fearing she just might faint.

Chapter 33

"That sounds like a real hoot, and I'm flattered as hell, but I can't leave Bar Harbor," Mona said. Outside the Harborside Hotel Rhonda Franklin stood in front of her while two bellhops loaded the trunk of a Lincoln Town Car with her luggage.

Rhonda nodded solemnly. "I understand. I just had to ask or I would always wonder."

Hayley stood off to the side watching the scene. She couldn't believe Rhonda had just asked Mona to come with her to New York, where she was returning to continue her hosting duties on *The Chat*, and to honor the remainder of her contract as the Redmond Meats spokesperson.

"The thing is, Ron, I could never give you what you want. And I got responsibilities. I still got a boatload of kids to raise and a deadbeat husband to feed."

Rhonda nodded, her lips quivering and her eyes brimming with tears. "You're a special woman, Mona Barnes. Your family needs to learn to appreciate you."

"Oh, they do in their own way. My kids made me

lobster-shaped pancakes for breakfast on Mother's Day. And my husband, well, my husband didn't exactly let me choose the movie on our date night, but he actually put his pants on and left the house to go to one, even though it was one of those stupid movies about cars that turn into robots, *Transponders* or *Transformers*, or whatever. It's not much, but it keeps me happy."

Rhonda leaned in and kissed Mona lightly on the cheek.

Mona smiled. "I had fun."

Hayley quietly stepped forward. The animal carrier she was holding was heavy and she was losing her grip. Inside, Pork Chop's snout was pressed against the metal grate on the latched door.

Rhonda happily accepted the carrier, cooed and kissed the potbellied pig's snout, and then handed it off to one of the bellhops, who slid the carrier in the backseat and strapped it in with an extended seat belt.

Rhonda turned back to Hayley. "Are you sure you want to do this?"

"He belongs with you, not me," Hayley said.

"Last chance to change your mind," Mona said.

Mona made no bones about her opinion. She thought Hayley was crazy to give Pork Chop to Rhonda Franklin and say good-bye to a cool twenty million dollars.

And Mona wasn't alone.

Liddy.

Randy.

Sergio.

Her kids, Dustin and Gemma.

Sal.

Hayley's mother in Florida.

They all thought she was crazy.

Her only allies were Leroy and Blueberry, who made it very clear they wanted that pig out of the house, and never wanted to lay eyes on it ever again.

Hayley's friends and family spent the better part of two days trying to talk her out of it. But Hayley had already made peace with the decision. She had no emotional connection with Pork Chop. She was his guardian only in the strictest sense of the word.

But Rhonda Franklin was another story. She adored Pork Chop. And he loved her.

It wasn't only the perfect match.

It was the right match.

And Hayley knew in her heart that Rhonda would do right by him, and make sure Pork Chop was as happy as, say, a pig in mud.

Rhonda already had a fortune. She didn't need the twenty million and had no desire to keep it. Hayley knew she had made the correct decision when Rhonda promised to donate the money to her favorite animal charities, which was a cause Hayley was passionate about ever since she was a little girl.

So no big mansions or yachts or lavish vacations in the French Riviera were in her immediate future, but hey, you never know what life may bring.

Rhonda hugged Hayley, took one last misty-eyed look at Mona, and then donned dark glasses to hide her tears and slid into the backseat of the Town Car. The driver shut the door and got into the driver's seat and they sped away to the Bar Harbor airport.

"Well, we'll always have one thing in common," Mona said.

"What's that?"

"We both waved good-bye to a rich and famous lifestyle. All you had to do was babysit a pig, and all I had to do was be Rhonda's girlfriend."

Hayley put her arm around Mona. "We both did the right thing."

"You think so? I'm not so sure."

"In any event, we also have one more thing in common."

"What's that?"

"After a day like this, we could both use a drink."

Hayley, with her arm still around Mona's shoulder, steered her to the left and inside the Harborside Hotel toward the bar.

Chapter 34

She could tell Leroy sensed something was wrong.

Hayley was gently stroking his fur just the way she always did, but there was tension in her fingers.

Her whole body, in fact.

Leroy's head was resting on her lap. He gazed up at her.

Even Blueberry, who usually took no notice of anything other than what directly affected him, had stopped licking himself across the room near the television and watched Hayley curiously.

She was trying hard not to cry.

She didn't want to collapse into a hysterical mess at this moment.

Not when Aaron was seated next to her on the couch where he had just broken up with her.

"I've been trying to have this conversation for a while now, Hayley. These months together have been wonderful. I don't think I've ever laughed so hard or enjoyed someone's company so much. . . ."

"But . . ."

"But I think we both feel the same way. Deep

down, on some level, we both feel that we're not meant for each other."

He was right.

But it didn't make it any easier to hear.

"You know, the funny thing is, for a while there I thought you were going to propose. . . ."

"What?"

She felt foolish bringing it up. It seemed so silly now.

"Liddy saw you looking at rings at a jewelry shop."

"Oh, that. It was a class ring. I was showing the owner a few scratches on it. I wanted to get it buffed and polished because I have a reunion coming up."

"I knew it had to be something like that. You know, Liddy; she's always spinning drama out of nothing. . . ." she said, her voice trailing off.

They sat in silence for another minute. Leroy licked her fingers. He was letting her know he was there for her.

Or maybe it was just the fried chicken she had eaten for dinner.

"Tell me something," Aaron said, taking a deep breath. "If I had proposed, would you have said yes?"

This was not something Hayley had contemplated. She just sat there wondering.

"I thought so. Your hesitation tells me I've done the right thing." Aaron stood up. "I better go."

Hayley picked up Leroy and set him down on the couch, and then followed Aaron to the door.

"I wish nothing but the best for you, Hayley. I hope we can stay friends."

"Of course."

She knew what that meant.

A casual hello at the grocery store.

Maybe a friendly nod at a potluck supper.

A quick catch up at one of her pet's vet appointments.

But they would never have another quiet dinner, just the two of them, and they would no longer share intimate stories about their past, and they would never kiss and touch each other underneath the Christmas tree and get tinsel in their hair and laugh about it.

That chapter in their relationship was coming to a close.

Aaron gave her a soft peck on the cheek.

And then he turned and walked out of the house and he was gone.

She closed the door.

And then she let the waterworks begin.

She went upstairs to her bed and sobbed until she exhausted herself and fell into a deep sleep.

Chapter 35

Hayley couldn't believe her eyes.

She just stared at the front page story in the *Island Times*.

It was an in-depth report on the two murders committed by Felicity and Alan Chan, the homicidal husband and wife team who had just been indicted.

The story would live on for months through the trial and sentencing.

But the story itself wasn't what struck Hayley.

It was the byline.

Underneath the headline, just in front of the first paragraph, it read, "By Bruce Linney and Hayley Powell."

Bruce had given Hayley cowriting credit.

Hayley stood up from her desk and carried the paper through the back bull pen to Bruce's small, cramped office where he was on the phone.

He waved her inside with a smile and finished his conversation.

"Okay, Ben, you take care." He slammed down the phone. "That was Ben Hendricks, city editor at the

Boston Globe. He saw our article and was calling to say what a bang-up job we did."

"You did the job, Bruce. You wrote the entire article."

"But you solved the crime. I told you, Hayley. We make an unbeatable team."

"I have to admit, working with you didn't suck."

Bruce laughed. "I'll take that!"

"I just want to thank you for giving me credit. It was a nice gesture."

Bruce jumped up from his desk and came around. "I'm telling you, we should join forces more often. Together we could turn this paper around."

"I think it's time I go back to focusing on my cooking column," Hayley said.

"You're too modest. Anyway, thanks again for helping me out with a great story," Bruce said, giving Hayley a kiss on the cheek.

The exact same spot Aaron had kissed her the night before on his way out the door.

Except this one felt different.

This time her whole face was flushed with a warm feeling.

For a moment she worried it might be menopause.

But after doing the math, she was confident that she still had at least a few years before that would happen.

Then why was she feeling so hot and bothered?

Bruce took her by the shoulders. "You okay? You look a little weird."

"No, I'm fine," Hayley said, brushing him off and hurrying back to her desk, where she sat down and tried collecting herself.

If not menopause, then what?

Why did that kiss make her feel so flustered?
Did she actually have feelings for . . . ?
No.
Stop.
What a ridiculous notion.
That would be impossible.
Not him.
Not Bruce.
She pushed the thought right out of her mind.
For now . . .

Island Food & Spirits
by
Hayley Powell

The actress Rhonda Franklin asked
me to write a few words in today's
column about her dearest friend, Olivia
Redmond, who you all know recently
passed away. What you probably don't
know is that Olivia and I forged our
own friendship of sorts in the weeks
preceding her untimely death, and this
bond we shared over our love of bacon
has been very special to me.

I had heard of the famous Redmond
family as far back as I can remember.
They had a summer home here on our
island and were very much involved in
the community. I remember when I
was a little girl at a Fourth of July
parade, I was awestruck by the dancing
pieces of bacon and hamburgers and
hotdogs on top of the massive Redmond Meats float. In reality those
meats come to life were just local

actors dressed in costumes, but I was mesmerized nonetheless. They would toss all us kids packs of bacon-flavored chewing gum as they passed by. I also remember Olivia herself, a teenager at the time, sitting on a makeshift throne, smiling and waving at the crowd. I idolized her. She was the closest thing to a celebrity I had ever seen at the time. I knew nothing about her, but she was inspiring to me sitting so high on that float, on top of the world. It was only later, as an adult, that I really got to know the woman behind the myth in my mind.

Olivia's family was always very generous with the locals. It was no secret that all those hotdogs we consumed at the high school football and basketball games during the school year and that delicious crispy bacon we enjoyed at our church breakfast fund-raisers were donated by the Redmond family, a tradition Olivia carried on when she took over as the company's CEO after her father's passing. Kindness and generosity are two admirable qualities she possessed. But I recently learned something about Olivia from a mutual friend (all right, most of you know I'm talking about Mona Barnes) that put her in a whole new light.

Olivia loved animals as a child. She

befriended many of the cattle that grazed and grew on the Redmond family ranch even though from a very young age she was told the truth about her new friends, that they were being raised to feed many thousands of people in our country. She made it her mission to make sure those animals had the best life possible before they departed the farm. This innate caring on her part carried over into adulthood, and when Olivia went to work at the family company she overhauled many of the standard meat industry practices and focused on animal health and safety, taking a more organic and health conscious approach to how they raised their products, despite the initial impact it had on the family's profit margin.

She was a long way from when she was a little girl throwing lavish farewell parties for the cattle about to depart the family ranch when their time had come and inviting all her kindergarten friends over for hamburgers and hotdogs to say good-bye to all her cow friends. I know, I know. Those poor little kids probably didn't make the connection between the cattle they were playing with and those sizzling burgers on the grill, but cut them some slack, they were five years old.

It's tragic that we will no longer see

Olivia Redmond around town during the summer months, but her legacy will live on. And I hear Redmond Meats is planning an even bigger and more elaborate float than last year for the Fourth of July parade. I know I will be celebrating by raising a glass and saying thank you to Olivia for giving us so many varieties of meat for countless memorable meals for many years to come. She will most certainly live on in our memories, in our hearts, and in my case, in my cholesterol, according to my doctor.

Today's recipe, in honor of Olivia, combines pasta and bacon and garlic. These are a few of my favorite things, to quote Julie Andrews from one of my all time favorite movies, *The Sound of Music*.

And if you're wondering what cocktail to serve with this mouthwatering pasta dish, worry no more! I love to serve my Easy Bellini. Trust me, you won't be disappointed!

Easy Bellini

<u>Ingredients</u>
1 bottle peach schnapps, chilled
One bottle of Prosecco or a sparkling
    wine, chilled
    For one serving pour one ounce of

the chilled peach schnapps in a champagne glass, then fill the glass with your chilled Prosecco, serve and enjoy!

Rigatoni with Bacon and Peas

Ingredients

2½ cups of rigatoni
4 to 6 slices of bacon, chopped (I like more bacon)
1 small onion, chopped
2 to 3 cloves garlic, chopped
1 10-ounce package frozen peas
2 large tomatoes, cut into bite-size pieces
¼ cup freshly grated Parmesan cheese, more for serving
Kosher salt and ground black pepper to taste

Cook the pasta according to the directions on the package. Reserve one cup of the cooking water; drain.

Meanwhile cook the chopped bacon in a large skillet over medium heat, stirring occasionally, until it begins to crisp, 6 to 8 minutes. Add the onion, garlic, salt, and pepper. Cook while stirring occasionally, until the onion is soft, another 6 to 8 minutes. Add the tomatoes and cook until the sauce begins to thicken. Add the peas and

1/4 cup grated Parmesan and heat until warmed through, 3 or 4 minutes.

Add the prepared pasta and half of the reserved pasta water to the sauce and stir to coat the pasta. Use more of the cooking water if too thick.

Serve with the extra Parmesan and let your taste buds do the talking.

Index of Recipes

Please turn the page for an exciting sneak peek of
Lee Hollis's next Hayley Powell mystery

DEATH OF A PUMPKIN CARVER,

coming in September 2016!

Chapter 1

Halloween was Hayley's favorite day of the year, but it was also incredibly dangerous.

Especially to her waistline.

All that candy.

The peanut butter cups.

The candy corn.

The mini Milky Way bars.

Of course, every year without fail, she would stock up on every sweet imaginable, more than all the trick or treaters who showed up at her door could possibly stuff into their orange plastic pumpkins they carried around the neighborhood.

No, she was always left with a sweets overflow, and then she carefully hid her stash from the kids so she could gorge in peace when they weren't home.

As office manager at the Island Times newspaper, it was also her responsibility to have candy on hand in case any tiny ghosts and goblins and witches and werewolves might come into the office with their parents. She didn't want them to leave disappointed.

So as the office wall clock inched closer to five o'clock, which was her usual quitting time, her eyes never left the ceramic bowl of Gummy Bears that sat within her easy reach. She was always after her kids, even now as young adults, not to indulge in treats before dinner, but those chewy, delectable Gummy Bears seemed to be calling her and making her mouth water.

Just try one.

Yeah, right.

One.

When had she ever stopped at just one?

The next thing she knew she was scooping up a fistful, popping them three or four at a time in her mouth, closing her eyes, relishing in the fruity taste and jelly bean texture.

"Good night, Hayley," Bruce Linney said as he blew past her from the office bullpen, heading for the door.

Her mouth was full and she was chewing as fast as she could, but there were too many Gummy Bears in her mouth to swallow all at once, and she couldn't speak.

Bruce noticed her nonresponse and stopped at the door. "Everything all right?"

Hayley nodded.

Bruce took one look at the half empty Gummy Bear bowl and Hayley's bulging cheeks. It didn't take a detective to solve this one.

"Save some for the kids, okay, Hayley?"

Hayley narrowed her eyes and crinkled her nose making as mean a face as possible given the fact she could hardly voice her displeasure at the moment.

Bruce winked at her, smiled, and disappeared into the chilly autumn evening as orange and red leaves from the tree next to the office swirled around him.

Hayley's harsh opinion of crime reporter Bruce Linney had softened during the previous six or seven months. They had worked together on a story for the paper, and discovered, much to both their surprise, that they actually didn't despise each other. In fact, they worked rather well together, and even though on occasion they still rubbed each other the wrong way, at least the constant bickering and barrage of insults had quietly subsided.

Bruce had also started working out at the gym more, and had trimmed some of his belly fat and put on some muscle. It was impossible not to notice. Although Hayley always loved a nice bearish man she could hold onto, there was also an attitude shift in Bruce as he shed his excess weight and felt recharged physically. He seemed more confident, happier, more at peace. Which was a big change from when he was smoking and drinking and barking at Hayley for her insistence on encroaching into his crime solving territory.

No, the new Bruce was far more palatable.

And dare she say, sexy.

Hayley stuffed another handful of Gummy Bears in her coat pocket for the five minute ride home. She promised to prepare a healthy meal for herself and the kids tonight.

Whenever they got home.

She rarely saw them anymore.

Gemma was back home from the University of Maine in Orono continuing her work-study program at the office of Dr. Aaron Palmer, Hayley's ex-boyfriend and town veterinarian, and Dustin, an aspiring filmmaker, was off wheeling and dealing, scouting locations and casting his next opus as if the small town of Bar Harbor was actually his own personal east coast version of Hollywood.

As Hayley pulled into her driveway, she chewed on her last Gummy Bear, which toppled out of her mouth into her lap as her jaw dropped.

She couldn't believe her eyes.

Right there on the front porch were two jack-o-lanterns that had not been there when she left for work this morning.

The kids hadn't been home all day. She knew that for a fact since she had spoken to both of them less than hour ago.

One of the pumpkins had been expertly carved into the face of Batman. The other was a dead on caricature of Harry Potter.

Batman was Dustin's favorite fictional character from childhood.

Harry Potter was Gemma's.

Hayley felt her heart beating faster, ready to burst out of her chest.

There was only one person in the world who could have left those jack-o-lanterns on the porch.

Her ex-husband Danny.

He used to carve those exact same drawings every year for the kids when they were little.

It was one of the few tasks he could be counted on to complete.

Hayley jumped out of her car and ran to the porch to inspect the jack-o-lanterns up close.

They were definitely Danny's handiwork.

Which could only mean one thing.

He was sending her a direct message.

He was letting her know he was back in town.

Which, in Hayley's mind, was hardly a good thing.

Because whenever Danny Powell showed up, trouble soon followed.

And Hayley had no clue at this point in time just how much trouble was ahead.

Big trouble.